# WereCat Fever

*Enchanted Mountain*

by

E.L. March

This is a work of fiction. Names, characters, places, and incidents are either the product of the author's imagination or are used fictitiously, and any resemblance to actual persons living or dead, business establishments, events, or locales, is entirely coincidental.

**WereCat Fever**



Contact Information: info@thewildrosepress.com

Cover Art by *Diana Carlile*

The Wild Rose Press, Inc.
PO Box 708
Adams Basin, NY 14410-0708

Visit us at www.thewildrosepress.com

Publishing History
First Scarlet Rose Edition, 2019
Print ISBN 978-1-5092-2859-1
Digital ISBN 978-1-5092-2860-7

Published in the United States of America

**Reunions can be maddeningly infuriating, sexually satisfying...and quite dangerous.**

Sitting astride his horse, Bryan Cauldwell watched the ranch house with mixed emotions. The only woman he'd ever loved should be reading his email by now, and he couldn't help wondering how it was affecting her. If she ever felt anything for him, her insides would be as churned up as his were.

Suddenly, there was the sound of a loud crash, followed by some unladylike cursing, a thud, and something else shattering. Then he heard more cursing and silence.

*"I guess she got the message,"* Hunter thought. The mountain lion sat as still as stone with only his tail flipping back and forth effortlessly. Then Bryan's brother stretched, yawning, bored.

"I guess so."

*"Are we going to head down there?"* Hunter asked.

"I'd rather give her a few minutes to digest the message before I walk into her fist."

Hunter's huge canines flashed in the sunlight. "*Good thinking*." He expressed the thought with a little humor that Bryan didn't miss. "*So, I take it you don't think she'll be glad to see you now that she knows you're still alive and well. She is your mate, after all.*"

## Dedication

To My Little Snow Leopard

*Author Acknowledgments*

Thank you to those who enjoy the worlds I write…

# Chapter One

*Wilding's Plain, Colorado*

While Lacey Hampton studied the huge Colorado night sky, she waited for Bryan. She permitted herself the luxury of relaxing in the roiling waters of the quiet grotto, trying to settle her nerves. The spring soothed out the kinks and tension in her muscles. With the exception of a single thin strip of cloud crossing the waning full moon, the sky was brilliantly clear. The stars were no more than glitter sprinkled on a black backdrop.

"Lady, you look mighty tempting sprawled out here in these bubbles," Bryan whispered.

She jumped. His unexpected words and his breath at her ear took her by surprise. His deep, raspy chuckle told her the reaction was exactly the one he expected.

"Oh, you…" The reaction sent water splashing everywhere, especially all over him.

A shiver of anticipation ran down her spine, and yet her emotions remained bittersweet. Tomorrow he'd be leaving and wouldn't be back until the day after his graduation, and they still hadn't settled anything about their future. Besides, where would they go if she could go away with him? Her Master's program couldn't be postponed, and he hadn't made up his mind about law school, yet. Lacey closed her eyes and let out a sigh.

For now, she wouldn't think about Monday. Tonight she had one last chance to give Bryan a memory he'd never forget, and the grotto was the perfect place to enact her plan. Tonight she intended to worship his body the way he worshiped hers. She only hoped the memory would be enough to keep them both satisfied until he graduated.

He walked around to the smooth, rocky ledge and sat with that same graceful silence then hushed her with a mind-blowing kiss. His soft lips pressed hers open—his tongue so demanding and possessive, she forgot the question she wanted to ask.

When he finally released her, Lacey noticed he was just as affected as she was.

"H–how did you manage to get back here so quietly? I heard you at the cave entrance—"

"That was MacBride." He paused and inhaled several more times before he answered. There was a definite huskiness in his voice. "Thomas left the Jeep and took the horses back to your place for me."

"Don't let me forget to thank him for being a good neighbor."

Thomas MacBride had moved into the house on the ranch down the road from Lacey's when she was about three. They shared a kiddie pool naked a few summers and a friendship after that. When her father added Bryan to their weekend fishing trips, the three became inseparable.

No one mentioned the bruises or the way Bryan's stepmother began undermining his relationship with his father after Tory was born. Lacey's dad was Cauldwell's foreman, so they all kept their mouths shut and tried to protect Bryan. Later, when she and Bryan started dating, Thomas kept them off old man Cauldwell's radar.

"He's going out with Candace Holmes for me." Bryan wrapped an arm around her shoulder and pulled her into his embrace. "The arrangement is symbiotic. He's been trying to get in her pants all year, so consider him thanked," he said and pressed his mouth to hers before she could laugh.

The kiss deepened as he thrust his tongue inside her welcoming mouth and the laugh disappeared. Bryan's action felt like a claiming, as if he was branding himself on her, and as always, his hunger spread through her leaving her breathless and needy for him. The sound of her heart beating in her ears was so loud it drowned out the quiet sounds of nature.

Whatever had been ailing Bryan, what she had planned was sure to distract him. Something was bothering him besides the fever he came home with, and he wasn't saying what. To make matters worse, Lacey hadn't been able to wheedle it out of him.

Every time she thought about the plan she devised, heat melted her insides, reminding her how she'd be pleasing all of him in just that way, shortly.

His hands ran over her naked shoulders and dipped beneath the bubbles, but Lacey anticipated them as they skimmed down her sides and back up, cupping her breasts.

"You have the most perfect breasts." His thumbs brushed back and forth across her nipples, and when they peaked, he feathered the backs of his hands over them, and then proceeded to explore the rest of her body.

Her skin shivered with anticipation.

"I love the way you react to my touch."

Hey, she loved reacting. Tonight she was going to turn the experience around and surprise him. She ran her tongue over her lips and smiled. Just thinking about tasting him made her hot. Lacey brought her finger to her lips and sucked, holding back a nervous giggle. If she didn't start thinking like a seductress, she was going to blow the plan.

The beneficial effect of the warm water soothed her concerns. At the same time, the natural, effervescent mineral springs stimulated her longing for Bryan's touch. The bubbles caressed her skin, teasing her most intimate places, and the sensation on her hypersensitive skin forced her breath to catch.

"You like this, don't you?" he asked, swirling a finger in circles around her nipple. "Open your legs wider so the bubbles hit all your highly sensitive spots."

She released an unexpected gasp and relaxed into the delightful experience. It felt almost as good as when he used his tongue on her.

Almost… Nothing was quite as good as having his talented mouth and hands exploring her body. Imagining the way he would explore those same sensitive nerves when he touched her made her moan.

"Hurry up." Lacey tugged at him. "Take your clothes off and get in."

"Mmm." Bryan chuckled, returning to tease the tip of her nipple with a gentle pinch. "What's the rush?"

God, he knew just where to touch her. She couldn't wait to show him what she planned.

"Selfish, I guess. I want you inside me as often as possible before you leave."

With an urgency Lacey didn't miss, he rolled the

black T-shirt up and over his broad shoulders. Every lean muscle rippled with the effort.

"Whoa! I swear you're bigger than you were at spring break. What are they feeding you down there?"

He grinned and flexed a few muscles before he cupped his groin. "I'm growing. But it's not the food that's doing it."

"Oh! No, kidding…" Lacey opened her eyes wide and paused when she saw the size of the bulge in his jeans. She'd had her hands on him and felt him inside her often enough to know this was different. The sight made her mouth water. As soon as she got her hands on him she was going to trace each defining line with her fingers, first fanning her hands across his chest and every inch of that golden skin and then with her tongue.

"You'll get no objection from me. If I had my way, I'd be balls deep inside you all the time."

"Sounds like an interesting plan if we can take a break every now and again to eat." Looking at the growing bulge, she wasn't sure how much of him she could take in her mouth, but she couldn't give up her plan without trying. With a renewed enthusiasm, she decided to give him her best effort.

Then he turned around to toe off his boots and socks.

While his back was to her, she said, "Bryan, I have a surprise." She smiled and licked her lips just thinking about his reaction.

"What exactly do you have in mind?"

"Since you're leaving in the morning, I want to be in charge of pleasuring you tonight."

"I can't imagine you pleasuring me any more than you already do, Lace."

Still with his back to her, he stood up to undo his jeans. Anticipation raced through her. Waiting to see the rest of him unwrapped was like waiting to open a birthday present. It was almost better than heated foreplay when he began undoing his pants. His biceps flexed. He unzipped and pushed the jeans over his hips and down his legs. His ass and thighs were powerfully built, and the fine hairs covering his skin were equally golden across his entire torso. She wanted him to turn around so she could see all of him.

He glanced over his shoulder.

"I've been thinking…" Her breath caught in her throat when he paused. "You know how you do those things to me with your mouth…?"

She noted how he seemed to stop breathing when he caught her admiring his ass. She didn't bother hiding the admiration from her expression.

"Uh huh," he said.

"Well, I want to do them to you."

Bryan froze in place with his hands on his hips as he glanced over his shoulder. Every muscle in his body tightened, and his groan sounded desperate.

Lacey inhaled when he whipped around to face her. Her gaze dropped and stayed focused on his groin. He was huge. Already hard, his cock stood proudly against his abdomen and jerked at her regard.

"Are you trying to kill me?" he asked incredulously at her.

"Not at all. I just want to make you happy."

She couldn't take her eyes off him. It had been a while since she'd seen him, but he'd filled out this year. Bryan was amazing when fully erect. The trail of downy hair leading from his chest to his groin shimmered in the reflection from the lantern. The patch at the base of his cock was slightly darker and thicker, a dark golden nest for his magnificent shaft.

When she tore her attention away from his cock to focus on his face, his grin was exactly what she expected—the cat that ate the canary—a total predator eyeing his prey.

"Lacey, you always make me happy." He glanced down at himself. "See how happy I am."

What had she been thinking? Whatever made her think she could seduce him for a change? "Bryan, merely looking at you turns my insides to hot molten lava. I'm ready to give in to you, and five minutes ago I was determined to resist until I wrestled control away from you. How else can I give you the same kind of pleasure you give me with your mouth?"

"I love you, Lacey," he said, softly. His erection grew larger while she admired him. "You please me in every way. But I'm warning you. If you take me in your mouth it'll be all over too soon."

There was no denying his reaction to her. "I love you, too, Bryan. Please let me show you how much for a change." She kept her attention on his torso and let out a long admiring sigh.

"Tell me. What do you want to do?" He raised an eyebrow in question, but she lowered her gaze and her voice. Her words escaped as a whispered sigh.

"I need to take your full length inside my mouth from crown to balls." She looked back up and made eye contact with him, ran her tongue over her lips, and swallowed in anticipation. "I want you to come in my mouth so I can taste you."

His eyes narrowed, the color darkening as he

responded with a slow shudder. He practically growled as he reached for her, releasing a rough breath as he dragged her body out of the water and brought their skin flesh to flesh. “You know the affect you have on me when you say things like that?”

She held her breath and nodded.

“I want to fuck those pretty lips of yours and then your tight little pussy.”

Donna was right. Apparently, men liked talking dirty.

When he tilted her chin so she had to look up at him, his next words sounded even more ragged. “Damn, it’s sexy as hell having you express how much you want me and exactly what you want to do.”

“Know why I like saying things like that?” Her insides heated with pure satisfaction knowing she could be open with him in every way because he was willing to express his own vulnerability. It was hard for him to hold back physically and open up emotionally with his background. His family demanded too much of him, and she was his only outlet, a safe haven.

“I’ll bite.” Bryan asked, “Why?”

“’Cause it makes you hard. And when you’re hard, I want you so much I can’t breathe. Just thinking about you makes me hot. And when I can’t touch you, it’s torture.”

“Oh damn, Lacey. You have no idea how fucking much I want you.” His touch remained gentle, but his jaw tensed, the chorded muscles running down his neck tightening. “Sometimes so bad I think I need you more than air. Every minute of every day—nothing else matters, except you.” The desperation in his words made her heart ache as he buried his face into the curve of her neck.

"Bryan, you were my first and I promise you'll be my only lover. There's nothing I won't do to please you."

Lacey smiled to herself as he nibbled her neck. "Come in here so I can show you exactly how much I want you," she said.

He climbed in beside her, sank into the water, and, leaning his head back, sighed. "Okay. Come on. Show me."

"No. You need to sit up on the ledge so I can taste you."

He groaned but did as she asked. She lowered her lips to his cock and licked the pre-cum pearling thickly at his opening. He relaxed beneath her hands and allowed himself to enjoy her decadent mouth—the way she sucked him in and licked up his length like he was dessert. She twirled her tongue across the mushroomed tip, teasing the tiny opening, and moaned around it, sending the vibration straight to his balls.

Kneeling before him as if she were idolizing him, the expression on her face seemed almost reverent. Bryan forced himself to hold back. He stopped the threatening orgasm at the last minute, but more pre-cum seeped from his cock, plentiful enough for a few drops to run down his shaft. She shook off his hands and buried her face back in his lap, licking the excess from his shaft as if it was a melting ice cream cone.

Watching her feast on him was the most erotic thing Bryan had ever seen until she took his pulsing tip between her lips and sucked him deep, tilting her head back for better access. When she leaned back and took his rigid member down her throat, he couldn't resist arching his hips.

He almost lost it. Inhaling and exhaling, using every ounce of self-control he had left, he prevented himself from driving himself down her throat. Bryan needed to thrust, wanted to pump and come in Lacey's mouth more than he ever wanted anything. Except, he wanted her squirming beneath him, with his cock buried deep inside her tight pussy, as she pulsed around him, her hot honey dripping over him when he came.

The warning sizzle ran up his spine. "Lacey…" he moaned.

Taking her head in his hands, he moved, pulling out of her tempting mouth.

"No more."

He shuddered, holding back his orgasm, refusing to ejaculate, yet. As much as he wanted to prolong this pleasure, he realized he was on a dangerous edge, ready to explode with the tiniest provocation.

She released him, lifted her chin, and licked her lips with a devilish smile on her lips. "Am I pleasing you?"

"Oh, yeah," he grunted. Barely able to prevent his climax, his voice had gone deep and guttural with desire. He hardly recognized it as his own. "Any more pleasure and I won't be able to hold back."

"Don't. I want you to lose control. I want you to come in my mouth." Her moist, plump lips pouted. The expression on her face and her words had Bryan rethinking. She almost made him disregard his earlier intensions and his images of coming inside her.

"Wait." He held her face and stilled her, inhaling deeply, pausing for a moment, before he took another deep breath. "Where the hell did you learn how to—?"

"Donna gave me some books to read. And…I, uh, practiced on…various foods. Popsicles and cucumbers." She glanced down at his cock. "Nothing as big or as delicious as this."

"Donna? Remind me to thank her." The vision of Lacey's mouth on him, her face buried in his groin, and the enthusiastic way she lapped up his pre-cum, left no doubt she enjoyed his taste and his scent. "Do you have any idea how much it pleases me to know you enjoy taking me in your mouth?" Knowing she liked giving head made Bryan's cock even harder, if it was possible.

She shook her head.

"It does! God, how I'm looking forward to years and years of satisfying BJ's, babe. But for now, this is much too overwhelming for me. It's been way too long since we've made love, and I can't wait to be inside you."

Her tongue whipped out to wet her lips before she bit down on her lower lip. "Bryan, let me finish this."

He almost caved. The idea made his balls tighten again. He fought back the tingling sensation, signaling his readiness.

"You have no idea how appealing that is, but no. I want to be inside you with your tight pussy milking my cock when I come. After, I'll let you coax me into another erection with your mouth. How does that sound?"

Her eyes narrowed on him, and her pink, swollen lips turned down into another pout. They were shiny, wet, and oh so damn tempting. "Promise?"

"Yes. Later." He smoothed Lacey's hair and massaged her neck, then tilted her head up to look into her eyes. "Lacey," he said, "as appealing as coming in your sweet mouth seems, this first time tonight, I want to be buried inside you. I want your tight, wet heat surrounding me when I come."

"You almost came, didn't you? You almost lost that rigid control."

"Hell, yeah," Bryan said.

Lacey grinned from ear to ear when he nodded and she let out a sigh. "Okay. This time," she said with her husky voice. "But, next time I get to swallow."

He grabbed his cock away from her when his balls clutched. "Stand," he said, helping her off her knees.

Water dripped from her breasts like tiny teardrops. So lovely. So tempting. He couldn't resist catching one on the edge of his forefinger and raising it to his lips.

"Lacey, I want to taste all of you. I need to suck these nipples while I explore your hot, pink pussy."

Her eyes glazed over with desire. Her lips were swollen from sucking cock like she'd done it hundreds of times, and yet this had been her first time. He kissed those lips—so pink, so moist, and, ah, so tempting—until she gasped for breath.

"Enough of these bubbles," he groaned and took her by her upper arms, pulling her closer. She giggled as he playfully tickled her. With one arm around her back and the other under her knees, he scooped her up, heading inside to the back of the cave where he'd made a bed out of blankets.

The tension in his body surrendered slowly as she touched him, and he returned touch for touch. He ran his hand down her neck, her shoulder, her breast, and paused.

"Your skin feels like silk. Mmm. Your nipples remind me of sweet summer berries." He licked one and watched as she writhed. “Did that send tongues of heat shooting straight to your clit?” She arched and nodded without answering. “Good,” he said. “I liked knowing your need is as great as my own.”

“Open up for me, Lacey.” He separated her petaled folds and searched until he found her most sensitive spot.

Lacey spread her legs farther apart to give him better access. Heat flooded her insides as he teased and probed until she couldn’t prevent the gasp.

Bryan gave her a satisfied grin before he bent his head to her center and sucked the nub that sent her over the edge screaming his name.

Although she’d been the one to initiate the offensive, he’d managed to turn it back on her. He took her deliberate seduction and turned it into a full-blown assault on her emotions as well as her senses.

Bryan settled between her hips and pressed his hard cock at her entrance. His hands moved at a pace her emotions couldn’t keep up with. She never felt so wonderful, so enriched or complete.

Sparks tingled across her skin and vibrations shot through her insides as he separated her folds with the tip. His erection at the juncture to her opening demanded her full attention. She arched seductively, offering herself up for him to take more. Lifting her hips, she watched his eyes as his length inched inside her. He slid into her waiting warmth as she accepted him with a sigh, holding him desperately against her body.

The muscles in his arms trembled as he held himself back and stared at her sex. He touched her clit, and she opened to receive more of his length. His fingers pressed and played with her nub as he filled her.

"You're beautiful. Perfect. I love seeing us joined like this," he murmured against her lips.

He started rocking into her, his cock stroking her inside, coaxing her, drawing her to him. "I'm coming," he warned as her orgasm exploded around him. Her internal spasms gripped him, and as she came, she forced his release with hers. When her climax ebbed, he collapsed on top of her, rolling her to the side as he clasped her tightly to his chest.

## Chapter Two

Lacey closed her eyes, blinking back the tears. What was the matter with her? Swallowing the lump in her throat, she swore she wouldn't cry. The separations were like enduring time in limbo. Only existence. Nothing more than an empty void until Bryan returned and once again held her in his arms.

Six more weeks.

After handling the long distance relationship thing for four years, surely another few weeks wouldn't be unbearable. What would being apart for six more weeks mean when they had a lifetime of being together to look forward to? In the larger view? Nothing. But every time she waved good-bye to him, she worried it would be the last—that this time his family would find a way to keep them apart.

"What's going on? You've been withdrawn," Lacey said.

"Withdrawn? I'm still inside you. And semi-hard, too." He laughed and angled his cock thrusting it deeper inside her to prove it.

"Not like that." Her lips curled up, and she gripped his hips with both legs, unwilling to let him go. "Tell me honestly. Are you all right?"

"Eh, it's nothing."

He tried to look away, but Lacey held his face with both hands. She stared him down and traced her tongue across his lips. “Tell me.”

“Not sleeping well. I’ve been having strange dreams lately. Not feeling myself—”

“How?”

“Forget it. It’s nothing. I had a fever. Like I said, nightmares. I’m feeling better.” He flipped her to her back and rode her. His fingers teased one nipple as his other hand slipped between their bodies where he joined her. “You’re what I needed this weekend.”

She stilled both hands. “What sort of fevers and nightmares?”

“You’re not going to let this go, are you?”

She shook her head. He flopped to his back, spread-eagled beside her. His cock was erect and shiny with their mixed juices. But he stared up, focused on the cave ceiling. She rolled and straddled him so he had to look at her.

“Spit it out.”

“The nightmares were strange, really violent, and then there was the one blackout. I woke up in the desert one morning, naked.” He raised his hand. “And don’t say it. I hadn’t been drinking.”

“Tell me you didn’t have a naked girl with you and I’ll let you live.” She glared, teasing him.

“Hell, no—no girl!” he said, sounding shocked she would even tease him.

She wasn’t worried. Jealousy never played a role in their relationship. Even though they were apart so often, a part of him always felt like it remained with her.

“Babe, you know there’s no one for me besides you.”

He took her hand in his and wove their fingers together as he stared up at her. The night sounds grew silent before he spoke again and Lacey waited.

"When I woke, I had blood on my hands and couldn't remember how I'd gotten there."

"My God, Bryan!" She jumped off him, sat up, and inspected him as if she hadn't noticed if he'd been injured before now. There was nothing. Shock sucked the air out of her. "Were you hurt?"

"No. I was fine. That was the strange part. I had a few scratches, but not enough to account for so much blood. And they healed up remarkably fast."

"There was no one around?"

"No, nobody and nothing to hint at what happened. I couldn't remember anything after I went to bed in my apartment that night." He ran a hand over his forehead and then through his hair. "I'm worried."

Honestly, so was she. "Did you see Doc?"

"Yeah, Thursday. He ran some tests. Wanted to run more, but there's no time."

"Make the time—"

"Not this trip, babe. After graduation, when I get back, I'll see him."

"Bryan, if anything like that happens again, go to the infirmary. Don't take any chances."

"Okay." He cupped her cheek. "I'm not sure what's happening to me. All that blood. It scared me. I… What if…? I could have done something really bad while I was blacked out."

"No. Not you. There has to be some reasonable explanation."

"What if I'm dangerous?"

"Don't be ridiculous. You're not dangerous. You could have been attacked by an animal, fought back and wounded it." Lacey held on to his wrists and stared deep into his eyes. "I'm not afraid of you, Bryan. You'd never purposely hurt anyone, especially not me."

She touched her lips to his and stared deep into his eyes, pressing her breasts against his chest to distract him. He wrapped his arms around her and pulled her back under him. The distraction worked.

"Ahh," he moaned. "Between you and the mineral springs, I'm finally feeling better. Lacey, you've become a part of me, my soul—balancing me and grounding me."

With her forehead pressed to his, she rubbed her thumb across his lips with one hand and cupped his hard jaw with her other, refusing to allow him to draw away. She was determined to hold his attention. Angling her lips to touch his and softly mingling their breath, she ran her tongue inside his mouth, testing, and tangling her tongue with his until she felt his pulse kick up and his respiration increase.

Bryan's heart raced. Maybe the pressure of school was finally getting to him, he thought. He allowed Lacey's scent to seduce him and turned control of the kiss over to her for the moment. Her mouth was hot and hungry for him. She tasted sweet, fresh, and wild.

When her breath hitched in her throat, he couldn't take any more. He ravaged her lips and took back control, deepening the kiss, taking it from sensual to erotic.

"Yeah, this was what I needed. Sexual recreation and mindless pleasure…and you."

His hands moved from where they rested lightly at her waist to a slow ascent up her sides while his thumbs drew lazy circles on the underside of each breast. He nibbled her neck and held her closely against his body, making her feel loved and cherished.

"You smell so good, Lacey." He inhaled her scent, murmuring against her skin. Touching her—stirring her feelings.

The difference in their lovemaking this time shocked her. She could mark the exact moment when he accepted their feelings for each other and silently pledged himself to her with his body. Something shifted inside her as she held him tightly. The earth moved beneath her and something inside her heart stirred. Her fingers feathered across his chest, feeling his heart beating beneath her hand in time to hers.

Every movement between them was a loving caress, a blending of two beings, a mating of like hearts, a merging of two souls. How could she feel like this, knowing his family would never accept her?

A sudden sadness enveloped her.

With a serious look of his own, he studied her expression. "Stay with me, Lacey. Don't go down the dark road."

As always, he somehow managed to sense her concern.

"I'm with you." She smiled, knowing she'd never be able to hide her distress from him.

"Lace, I pledge myself to you completely, right now. I want to yield completely to our passion and our love, forever. I want you too much to lose you."

"You're not going to lose me, Bryan. Never."

"You're right." He winked and then whispered in her ear, "Only six more weeks, Lacey girl and I'll be back to marry you."

"Marry! But, your father—"

"Forget about my father. I have."

"He'll never let it happen." Lacey sighed. Her throat felt too tight to swallow. The tears burned her eyes. "He'll find a way to stop us."

"No one can stop us now." With those words, he took his pinky ring off his finger and placed it on the middle finger of her left hand. It was too big, but her heart swelled with hope.

"Will you marry me, Lacey?"

# Chapter Three

*Five Years Later*

The Colorado heat didn't help Lacey's mood. With hot days already upon them, she had nothing to look forward to other than more blazing days and even hotter nights. In past years, she refused to wallow in the funk she usually felt whenever summer rolled around, marking the week her life changed forever. She learned to block her feelings to protect them. But with the town's Diamond Jubilee happening this weekend, it was impossible not to think about Bryan Cauldwell. Yes, the town was named for his family. They owned damned near everything in these parts, but not her.

Four years, eleven months, and twenty-eight days ago, Bryan failed to show up for their rendezvous. Disappointment eventually turned to disillusionment, followed by concern, and eventually a broken heart. Then, things went from bad to worse.

The last week—that was how she came to think of that week that ended with her entire life in upheaval. Bryan had been ready to graduate and she was three years into a five-year master's research program at the local university. He'd asked her to marry him and then disappeared.

The sound of Thomas's jeep stopping in front the house pulled her out of her thoughts.

Keiran's voice shouted out, "Hey, Tommy, how are you? Tell Lace I'm done with the lessons today and I'll be in in a few minutes."

A man's boots sounded on the wooden steps. Long strides, confident. Thomas.

"Humph. That's Thomas to you, Squirt."

*Nothing changes.* Lacey heard the screen door open and slam shut.

"Lace, hope you're not decent. I'm coming in." Thomas yelled from the front door. "Where are you?"

He'd find her. He always did.

Lacey smiled and sat down. She glanced at the picture on her desk. With a gentle touch, she ran a finger over the glass, pausing beside the image of her father's face. Her favorite picture showed them together, his arm slung over her shoulder as if they were the best buddies in the world. A fifteen-year-old version of Lacey grinned up at her father—her smile spread from ear to ear. The fish she held up with his help was almost as big as she was.

"There you are, hon. How are you feeling?" Thomas asked as his large presence filled the den. "Fever any better?"

She glanced up at her best friend, looked back at the picture, and lied. "Fine."

"Liar." He glanced at the picture.

"Why ask?" She kept the placid expression fixed on her face to keep Thomas from seeing how upset she really was.

"I'm getting the sweet tea. You're going to join me, right? I suppose Squirt will expect me to fix her a glass, too. I'll bring a tray. After she leaves"—he nodded to the picture—"we'll talk." He never missed anything where she was concerned.

Keiran stomped her boots on the porch and wiped them off before coming in. “Are you in the den?”

“Yup. Thomas is bringing tea. Sit. And thanks for taking my lessons this week.”

“The MacAllen girl is sweet and Daniel is a charmer. It was no trouble.”

Keiran was easygoing and petite. The handicapped kids identified with her because she was so tiny.

“Oh, darlin’, you’re still not feeling well, are you? And you’ve worked harder than anyone on the jubilee committee.”

She glanced at the photo on the desk and asked, “You taking a walk down memory lane? With everyone returning this weekend, it must be hard on you.”

“If I recall correctly, Bryan was the one who took that picture of me and Dad. The starry-eyed crush I developed on Bryan started shortly after school let out for the summer, but it was another full year before he noticed me.”

The memories made Lacey’s lip twitch in spite of the painful memory.

“Oh, he noticed you before then all right,” Keiran said. “He made every excuse and took every opportunity to be wherever you were.”

“Who?” Thomas came in and put the tray on the coffee table.

“We’re talking about how Bryan wouldn’t ask Lacey out even though he couldn’t stay away from her.”

“Guys are like that,” Thomas said. “We have no idea what to say once the blood rushes to our cocks.”

“Nice imagery,” Lacey said.

“One minute you’re invisible and the next minute you grow boobs and we turn into stalkers with drool on our lips.” Thomas could really put the comic book version into words.

“Anyone ever tell you, you have a disgusting way with words?” Lacey laughed.

“But he’s right.” Keiran nodded. “I remember several guys drooling over Lacey’s boobs the year they popped up.”

“In the beginning, things with Bryan were weird. We’d been good friends up until then. Our old, easy friendship turned into an awkward teenage relationship while we wrestled with our feelings. Thank goodness Thomas came to the rescue.”

What she didn’t say was that, despite the Cauldwells pushing Bryan at every eligible country club deb through high school and college, he’d remained loyal to her, defying his father to the bitter end.

“Well, if it wasn’t for Thomas, you two never could have hidden your relationship from old man Cauldwell.”

Thomas leaned back in the recliner and grunted. “Remember when that weasel brother of his tried to catch Bryan sneaking over to see you. Using me for cover was brilliant. I savored that goodnight kiss for years.”

“Get over it. It worked.” Lacey sipped her tea and tried to discuss her past objectively through the old, dull pain.

“Tory was always jealous of Bryan,” Keiran said. “He said all those horrible things because you wouldn’t go out with him. Like that’s the way to a girl’s heart.

Lacey, I don't know how you survived."

"Neither do I. I think I was in shock after my father died. But I had Thomas and you and Donna. You all rallied round like my own protective superheroes."

"I like that," Thomas said. "Superheroes, huh?"

"Since we're finally talking about this. Did any of you ever think Bryan had anything to do with my father's death, like Tory insinuated?"

Keiran and Thomas glanced silently at each other. Thomas pushed the recliner up and walked over to Lacey. He got down on one knee so he was eye level with her and said, "No, we didn't. Whatever happened, Bryan never would have hurt your dad."

"Even the sheriff said it was a wild animal attack."

"Don't you think Bryan going missing, and then having several of Cauldwell's men find my father dead out near the caves, was suspicious? We went there all the time."

Thomas got up and paced. "If anything, it looked like a setup."

Lacey shook her head. As bad as that week had been, she never envisioned it ending that way.

"Something bothering you, Lacey?" Keiran asked.

"Nothing really. It's just, after all this time, I still have so many unanswered questions. I thought maybe you guys had some thoughts. I know you're afraid I'm too fragile to discuss this—"

"No, never fragile," Thomas said. "Hurt, yes. We're your friends and we see how painful it all is…still."

Keiran took Lacey's hand. "You finished that master's program and went on to earn a PhD in record time, but you substituted work for living. You haven't moved on with your life. Those unresolved issues keep you trapped in the past. I think it'll be good to discuss them."

"Thank you, Dr. Keiran." Lacey patted her friend's hand in return and chuckled. "You really got something out of that Psych 101 class."

"Keiran's right, Lace."

"I know she is," Lacey admitted. That week forced her to mature fast. She learned a few of life's lessons the hard way. One—love doesn't last forever—and two—you can survive without a heart. But one thing she needed was answers. She was sick and, thinking back, it was all related.

"Although I may never find answers to all my questions, I want to start looking. Thomas is right. I need closure."

Thomas, as always, just said, "Count me in."

"What do you need from us?" Keiran asked.

"I'm not sure, but I trust your instincts. Talk to people this weekend. There will be friends here we haven't seen for a while. Maybe they remember something from back then. We need to pick their brains."

"What exactly are we looking for?" Thomas asked.

"Information about the days before or after that week." Lacey was frustrated. "I'm a biologist, not a detective, Thomas. I know how to do research studies, but I'm not sure how to go about a cold case investigation. Maybe it's the same."

"Squirt can ask Jack. He's a detective with the sheriff's department. Maybe he'll help."

Lacey's research for the Department of Fish and Wildlife took up her life outside the ranch. She had friends and a small social life. Hell, she wasn't a martyr. She wanted her life back. There were things she could deal with and some things she couldn't. Now she wanted answers.

Reflection made her angry about all she'd lost. She turned the picture frame face down on her desk. There weren't many reminders of her father or Bryan left sitting around the house anymore.

Lacey sighed. "Only if we stay below the sheriff's radar. He'll be pissed if he finds out we're meddling and Jack's involved."

"We'll get Donna involved. You know she loves a good mystery." Thomas added, "And she'll be pissed as hell if we don't include her."

"Don't worry. I'll convince Jack. I have magical powers of persuasion where he's concerned." Keiran put her arms around Lacey. "I'm glad you've decided to take action. I suddenly feel empowered."

"Squirt, your level of enthusiasm is empowering." Thomas ruffled Keiran's short, dark hair. It didn't make any difference in her pixie-like appearance.

"Good. Now that we're all empowered, and that's all settled, let's talk about something else." Lacey blinked back happy tears and laughed. Moving forward with a plan felt like the right thing to do.

"We could talk about what's going on with your blood tests," Thomas said, cocking his head to one side, "but I'm not sure that's any more uplifting. You look like shit, girl."

"Thank you for mentioning it." Lacey smoothed out her hair. "Maybe it's because I feel worse today than yesterday."

"Drink your tea. Should I get your pills?" Keiran

jumped up.

Lacey looked at the grandfather clock and motioned for Keiran to sit. “In a minute. It’s almost time.”

“Are you documenting your symptoms like Doc suggested?” Thomas asked.

“Yes.” She grew testy thinking about her symptoms and Bryan. “I’m hot. I hate this time of year.”

“Is it the weather or is your fever back?” Thomas asked.

“I don’t know,” Lacey said on a sigh.

“Really?” Thomas knew just how to hold her feet to the fire. “What’s your temperature?”

“I haven’t taken it.” Lacey checked her temperature with the back of her hand. God, she was burning up. “Hot.”

“What kind of scientist documents data with a general adjective?” Thomas asked.

“I know it’s not very accurate, but I’m definitely hot,” she said.

“Then we better document your symptoms for Doc.” Keiran said.

“Fine. The thermometer in the kitchen drawer came with a chart. I’ll get it.”

“I’ll come with you,” Keiran said.

“Me, too,” said Thomas with a sarcastic lilt. Wearing a smirk, he rolled his eyes in Keiran’s direction as he led the way into the kitchen. “We’ll help.”

After rummaging through the contents of the junk drawer, Keiran announced, “I’ve got it.” Sure enough, she found the thermometer, chart, and a pen. Her expression looked like she'd found gold.

"You're so cute, Squirt. I love your exuberance."

Her voice dropped to a conspiratorial whisper. "I'm charting my own temperatures. Jack and I are trying to get pregnant."

"Whoa, did you need to share that?" Thomas cringed. "I'm picturing sex with a clinical detachment. I'm picturing scrubs with tie pants and nothing beneath… Okay, I'm feeling better."

"You are such a slut, Thomas. Keiran, ignore him."

"I am. Don't worry. I'm a pro at this." Keiran put the chart on the counter and rinsed the thermometer at the sink before she said, "Open, Lace. No talking."

"Well, this is one way to keep Lacey quiet." Thomas tickled her, and Lacey smacked his shoulder.

"Leave the patient alone," Keiran said. "The last time Lacey manifested these symptoms, Doc suspected she picked up something from the wild cats out at the sanctuary—like a virile form of cat scratch fever or something."

"Nothing turned up in her blood work back then."

"How did you know?"

"Good guess." Thomas looked uncomfortable.

"Well, they chalked it up to PMS, put her on birth control pills, and they worked until the brand was taken off the market five months ago. Her bouts with the abdominal cramps started again."

The thermometer beeped. Lacey took the thermometer out of her mouth and said, "Hello! I'm right here. Stop talking about me like I'm not."

"What's it say?" Keiran asked.

"102 degrees."

"That's not good, is it?" Thomas said.

"Nope. It's up from 101.5 degrees last month." Keiran announced after reading the chart.

Lacey wrote the new numbers and her symptoms on the chart then put her arms around her friends' shoulders. "Okay, time for you two to go home. I'm going to do paperwork and rest." As an afterthought, she reminded them, "Don't forget what I said about asking questions this weekend."

"We can take a hint." Keiran smiled and hugged Lacey. "Feel better."

"We'll see you tomorrow at the planning meeting, right?" Thomas started out the door, but stopped. "I'm just down the road if you need anything. Call me."

"I will. And Thomas? Ask Kirk if he has time to look at my AC this week?

"I'll look—"

"Thanks. But no thanks. Kirk said he would. You can take care of me, buddy." She kissed Thomas on the cheek. "Okay?"

"'Kay."

Lacey walked her friends to the door and waved as they left. This made the fifth month she'd been off the pills and the fourth month she'd been ill. Contraception hadn't been an issue since her libido disappeared with Bryan. But the hormones kept her symptoms away.

Doc Wells had no idea what was causing her illness. Her new symptoms and the old cramps began after the weak spells, nightmares, and changes in her vision. Those weren't her only symptoms, but if she ever put the others into words, someone would lock her up and throw away the key.

The doc had tried her on different medications and various doses, but, since coming off the hormones, nothing worked. At least she wasn't dizzy or blacking out again. Yet.

She took the prescription out of the cabinet, opened a cool bottle of water from the fridge, and poured out the pills Doc prescribed. The new medication eased the monthly abdominal cramps. She tossed back the medication and water in one big gulp. The pink pill kept the fever down and the other helped the cramps—a little.

She was afraid the old doctor was right. Until they identified the ailment, they could only treat the symptoms. Many of the symptoms started with the mountain lion scratch. But they'd have to wait on the CDC. The results from last month's blood tests were due back any day.

The AC was on and blowing, but her forehead and upper lip still felt warm and damp. When she checked, the filter was clear. So, she pressed her hand over the AC vent. Yup, sure enough the force was strong, but not cool enough.

Kirk would take a look and correct anything that he found needed fixing. Normally she went to Thomas for help, but his brother was much handier with mechanical stuff. Thomas didn't normally like getting his hands dirty. He was more suited to the chain of nightclubs he owned in Denver, Dallas, and Austin. He ran the operations from Wilding's Plain while Kirk ran their cattle ranch. Their parents were still living, but moved to Arctic, Colorado after their father suffered a serious heart attack three years ago. Lacey still missed having them around for support.

Without the darn AC working up to snuff and with the dust from the drought blowing outside, she longed to find a cool place where she could rest in a safe spot outdoors. Sometimes her small ranch house felt too confining at night. Last month, she'd gone into the hills. Maybe she'd sleep in the old cave tonight. The cool damp mountain air would be a reprieve from the oppressive August heat, and she could soak off the day's dust along with a few aches and pains in the mineral spring out back.

Those unusual tracks she'd seen out there kept her in the mountains more than usual. Spending her days tracking undocumented animal prints for her book was a priority, but she had to admit the springs would feel good.

Before she could leave, there were a few things to wrap up with the committee before the town's diamond jubilee celebration. Damn Thomas for getting her involved. She had to check emails for additional, last-minute reservations to the country club gala and prepare the list for her friend, Donna, the Jubilee chairperson. As much as she wanted to ignore this celebration, her friends had dragged her in so deep there was no way of bowing out. Lacey was resigned to do her job and get this over with. Then she'd focus on her work and getting well.

****

Sitting astride his horse, Bryan Cauldwell watched the ranch house with mixed emotions. The only woman he'd ever loved should be reading his email by now, and he couldn't help wondering how it was affecting her. If she ever felt anything for him, her insides would be as churned up as his were.

Suddenly, there was the sound of a loud crash, followed by some unladylike cursing, a thud, and something else shattering. Then he heard more cursing and silence.

*"I guess she got the message,"* Hunter thought. The mountain lion sat as still as stone with only his tail flipping back and forth effortlessly. Then Bryan's brother stretched, yawning, bored.

"I guess so."

*"Are we going to head down there?"* Hunter asked.

"I'd rather give her a few minutes to digest the message before I walk into her fist."

Hunter's huge canines flashed in the sunlight. "*Good thinking*." He expressed the thought with a little humor that Bryan didn't miss. "*So, I take it you don't think she'll be glad to see you now that she knows you're still alive and well. She is your mate, after all."*

"Uh, she doesn't know that, yet. I'm going to have to do some pretty fancy talking to convince her she belongs with me. I have five years to make up to her."

*"I told you to return after I found out you were infected."*

"Is this the time for 'I-told-you-so's'? Really? I wasn't ready to condemn her to the risks and a life she knows nothing about."

*"No. You were the one who wanted to play hero and save her from herself. Too bad it didn't work out that way. Instead, you left your mate to fend for herself."*

"I was sick for three months—totally out of it. I didn't know those rogues stayed behind or anything about what happened to her father."

*"You would have if you hadn't been so stubborn. You should have checked on her before."*

"I did check. There was never any evidence she'd

been infected. She never showed any signs of changing until recently. Why do you think it took so long?"

*"I don't know. On average, male shifters go through the change later than females. But even some genetic shifters never change. In your case, the Were virus triggered your change. I still don't know why Lacey didn't show signs of the virus until recently. Maybe her metabolism is slow or she was on medication or something."*

"It doesn't matter. I couldn't interfere. She accomplished so much on her own. Finished college, got her degree. She has her career and the ranch. Hell, she could've had a normal life if it weren't for me."

*"Well, that option's off the table. When are you going to go down there and man up? Sorry...just an expression."*

"Hunter, you're not funny."

*"Really? You're probably right."*

"I'm trying to decide how to tell a woman her life is about to change forever. That almost everything the movies show about the paranormal world is true. How the hell is she going to react?"

*"I don't know, but you've had plenty of time to contemplate that over the last few years. It's not like you haven't been thinking about finding a way to convince her that this would be a good choice if she has to accept it. Don't forget, if the rogues sniff her out, she could be in real danger. So make up your mind. I'm getting hungry, and we don't know how much time she has left."*

"I know. That's why we're here." Bryan took his leather hat off and ran a hand through his hair. "I'm not leaving her side, whether she knows I'm here or not."

## Chapter Four

This weekend couldn't come and go quickly enough for Lacey's satisfaction—Sunday was the fifth anniversary of the day Bryan disappeared, the week before her father's body was discovered. The sheriff claimed he'd been killed by some wild animal, but none of the evidence pointed to any local species.

With a finger touch, Lacey clicked on her laptop to check the responses to the invitations for this coming weekend's events. The reminder date on the computer calendar may as well have been a big blinking neon sign blasting the approaching event.

Thomas talked her into joining the town council to get out and mingle. How she ended up assisting Donna, the chairman in charge, was still a mystery. She let out a hiss. Keiran and Donna always sided with Thomas when it came to what they believed was her well-being. If she ever found out who'd nominated her for the committee, she promised she'd wring one of her friends' necks. Thomas swore it wasn't him, but she believed he was the most likely culprit. When he insisted she delegated authority better than anyone, Lacey started thinking she'd been railroaded.

Stinker. Lacey smiled. He never envisioned finding out how good she was. Lacey ran him ragged with assignments for the jubilee and she tapped her finger on her desk thinking up more ways to get even with him.

He could meet with the local junior women's league tomorrow night. Half the women were single and hot for his scrumptious body and the other half were matchmakers, certain a man his age should be thinking about marriage. That would be pure torture since Thomas preferred variety, kinky sex, and ménages.

Her email inbox flashed, practically screaming at her. Ugh, more responses to sort through. Why did everyone wait until the last minute?

Rummaging through a few papers on top of her desk, she remembered the invitation list was inside the drawer. Right on top, with all the check marks, the list indicated who was coming and who was not. Her email notice pinged and she glanced back at the screen to see who else was responding.

One name jumped out of the rest. One name in the inbox had her insides quivering at the gall. The shock, after so long, sent her bolting forward in the chair. As a result, she knocked the glass vase off the desk. She cursed several very obscene epithets. Then suddenly the air seemed too thick to breathe, and her pulse pounded in her ears.

*He's alive. I knew it!*

For all she'd known, Bryan could have been killed along with her father. There'd been blood, but no body—no other evidence. Even so, there'd been another reason she'd known he was still alive. Even though his absence had left a hole inside her, the unusual connection they shared never changed. The bond still held her to him. If he'd been dead, she would have known it. Then at least she could've mourned him instead of cursing him.

A mixture of relief and regret settled over her when she couldn't stop the memories of their last days together. Everything came flooding back—the emotions with the memories. The memories included the weekend he'd come home sick to see the doc shortly before graduation. After a few days, his symptoms passed and his old libido returned with a vengeance, proving he was well enough to go back to school.

"I'll be back, soon," he'd said the next morning before he left and kissed the tears off her cheeks. "You'll be too busy with your finals to miss me." He'd chucked her under the chin and left.

*College, a couple of weeks, and then he'll graduate. Don't cry. It'll only be a little while before he's back for good...*

But that never happened.

This email was the first evidence he was alive. The first she'd heard from him since he'd waved good-bye to her as he drove out of town. They never found his car or him, and as far as she knew no one had heard from him again. Until now.

With a quick tap of the key, the header appeared. She stared and wondered…so many things. Her eyes flickered over the screen.

*To: LHampton@cauldwell.txmail.com*

*From: BCauldwell@arcticmail.co.com*

*Subject: Old friend*

Really? Old friend.

*Hi Lacey, hope you haven't forgotten me. We used to date some.*

Date? Ouch.

Which part stung most? Date some was what he called their relationship, and love of her life was the way she remembered him. More like "soul mate" than old friend.

Those curses she cried out in the nights after he disappeared seemed so much more appropriate now, knowing he chose his path. Damn him for breaking her heart. Damn him twice for returning. And damn him three times for being able to do it again.

The coffee cup from this morning sat innocently on her desk, awaiting her wrath. She let it fly, a substitute for the man she wanted to squash, the man she'd mistakenly believed in, the man who may have been involved with her father's death. The cup hit the library wall while she repeated those old curses and then some.

He'd stood her up after graduation, never showed up, never called, never wrote. Not only had he broken her heart, but the sheriff, his family, and the town went into an uproar looking for him.

What was he thinking to show up after all this time? All hell was going to break loose. For a moment she hoped he'd let someone other than her know he was returning. His father and the sheriff were going to crucify him—not to mention what she was going to do to him when she came face to face with the coward.

After five years was he suddenly thinking, "Oh, hey, wonder how that little Lacey is doing?" The email was supposed to be…what? A warning? "Get ready baby, I'm back?"

Yeah, like she'd been sitting around for five long years waiting for him to grace her with his presence.

Okay, so what if she had no life. He didn't have to know that.

Well, he had another thing coming.

*Maybe he'll break some law so the sheriff will lock*

*him up before I run into him.*

Everything churning through her mind turned into a collage of memories dredging up emotions she didn't want to experience. She remembered the football games and secret dates, picnics and moonlight. The kisses were so wonderful, she wondered if anything surpassed the way he made her feel when he touched her.

Lacey let her face fall into her hands. His disappearance had set off a chain of events she didn't want to relive. She lifted her head and stared at Bryan's message then shut her eyes. The words imprinted against her eyelids, and the shock was still too fresh in her mind. Just thinking about them brought the bitter pain back with the details.

Old man Cauldwell tried blaming her when Bryan, his oldest son, didn't return home from college. Tory, Bryan's half brother, the little son of a bitch, accused her of chasing him to ground until he couldn't stand the thought of returning. When she'd been too wounded emotionally to deal with them, her father stood up to the Cauldwells and took the heat for her. In the end, she believed her weakness cost her father his job and his life.

The sheriff claimed it was a wild animal attack, but Lacey believed otherwise. Bryan's father, the wealthiest rancher in the state, fired her dad the day before they found his body. To this day, Lacey was sure the Cauldwells were involved. If not Bryan, then his father had a part in her father's death or the cover-up. All the money in the world couldn't persuade her otherwise.

There was nothing she could have done back then. Knowing the older man's volatile relationship with Bryan made her suspect he had something to do with his own son's disappearance.

All those questions changed with this one email.

*Date some*?

Hardly. His father never let his son date his foreman's daughter. Fucking? Oh yeah! Fucking her was a different matter totally. That he might have accepted if he knew about it. Probably even would have preferred it. To that elitist S-O-B, she was okay to do in the dark or in the hills, but not good enough to bring out in public. He didn't want any negative attention brought to the family or his country club set.

It took years before she came to the realization that she and Bryan spent time together at school and sneaked off when they could. She believed those passionate I-love-you's he declared in moments of heated embraces because her own desperation wanted to. Now she recognized them for what they were to Bryan—a way to get in her pants. Over the last few years she'd grown to believe he wasn't any different from his father.

She looked out the window to the hills, the ones where she and Bryan went, where he'd lied to her, fucked her, and forgotten her.

Her eyes blurred, but she blinked away the self-pity.

There'd been nothing more in the email, nothing that mattered, anyway. Blah, blah, blah. No explanation. No apology. Merely statements that broached more questions.

*Don't believe for a minute that leaving wasn't as painful for me…*

She closed her eyes and swore she could hear his deep, rich voice murmuring the words in her head the way he once had.

More lies. And why now?

Even the prospect that he remembered her fondly made her wonder if he thought about her when he crawled under the sheets stark naked, the way he always slept. If he ran his hands down his tight abs, lowered them to his groin, and thought of her. Had he thought of her when he buried himself inside all those other women these last few years? Had he ever dreamed of her the way she had about him every night since the day they'd met?

Nothing hinted at an answer to the one burning question she would never ask. *How could you have loved me and done this to me?*

The only explanation she could come up with was that he'd lied, then and now. The knot in her throat threatened to choke her, making it hard to swallow. Her skin tingled, her eyes burned, and she glanced back at the computer, aching for more, for something she couldn't quite grasp.

The truth.

What happened to keep him away? And what happened to her father? If he didn't have the answers, she was sure he knew where to find them.

Blinking through the watery haze, she pressed *delete*, and closed her laptop. She needed to get out of the house before she did something irreparable…like cry. Because if she started, she wouldn't stop.

What she needed was something other than this heartache slicing through her breast. She needed fresh air. Open skies. The range. The hills.

And another emotion… *Anger.* That was an emotion that might settle her.

She dredged it up from repressed memories, savoring it, adding it to this most recent insult. When she recalled the pain, the red-hot anger was impossible to get past. Perhaps it would be enough to block her fear—fear that he'd find a way to get to her.

Anger always controlled the pain, but she'd need more to fight her feelings for Bryan.

Fortunately, she knew just where to find more of that anger. In their cave. If Bryan was coming to the diamond jubilee celebration, it would be the perfect opportunity for her to find retribution for her heartbreak, even if she never found it for her father's death. Lacey wanted a shot at bringing her old friend to his knees and gutting him the way his leaving had emotionally emptied her.

First, she'd find out what happened to her dad and make him confess to his father that she'd had nothing to do with his disappearance. Then she expected a massive apology.

If she managed to convey anything else, she'd make it clear she was over him. Because more than anything, she wanted to free herself of this caring, even if the thought of being without him was unbearable. A hot, shooting pain pierced her gut at the thought of the possibility. Honestly, her need was less about being free of him—it was more about wanting to be free of the inexplicable hold he had over her. She wanted that tie broken—wanted control over her emotions back. She had to break the emotional ties she felt to him. And he could never find out how often she thought about him, how much she wanted him.

Whenever she thought about missed opportunities for happiness, she thought about Bryan and how his disappearance had ruined her chance at a normal life. She learned how to compartmentalize her pain. She put Bryan behind door number one and locked it. But the unexpected email managed to shatter the lock and rip open the door. The memories flooded her defenses. The acute heartbreak returned, leaving her insides aching as if he'd left only yesterday.

How was she going to face him and block him from her emotions? He could never know how much he'd hurt her, never know how he still could—if she let him. She could never give him that power over her again.

She was going to ride into the hills and recall every tear she'd ever wasted over Bryan and the Cauldwells, find the anger she needed to face him, and then she'd figure out how to get even.

If he did still care, she'd give him a sample of the heartache. His damned email was five years too late. This time, when Bryan left, it would be his sorry ass wanting more.

*God help him.*

No, she thought. God help her.

## Chapter Five

Lacey Hampton hadn't changed much. If anything, she was more of everything Bryan remembered. Better.

He watched her tight, efficient body hop up onto the horse. She whipped the mare around as her loose, golden curls, pulled back in a clip, glistened and bounced around her shoulders.

She'd grown prettier, if that was possible, but looked stronger, more fit and yet, at the same time, more fragile than he remembered.

*Fragile.*

The word formed in his mind as if Hunter had actually spoken it. Not possible since Hunter was presently purring contentedly in the sun, still in his mountain lion form. He lounged on the rock above Bryan and his horse as if he didn't have a care in the world. If his tail wasn't flipping with interest as he watched Lacey ride off, he wouldn't have known the big cat was alive.

Hunter's interest made Bryan turn deadly still, jealousy pulling at him as his brother studied the woman he was bound to. He shook off the irrational thoughts and explained what it was that fooled people about Lacey.

"She's not fragile. Don't believe that for a minute. Everyone underestimates her. She's competent, sexy, smart—"

*"Must be if she handles all this land, works at the university, and looks like a wood nymph."*

"Looks can be deceiving."

*"Yeah, don't we know that?"*

His thoughts returned to the reason he was here. "Hell, she's more than I deserve."

*"Mmm, probably."*

Bryan glanced over his shoulder and shrugged at the golden cat who sounded more attentive than he looked. It appeared nothing concerned him until he noticed a sharp glint in the cat's eyes.

Bryan forced back the jealousy again. The sudden urge to follow Lacey, as he had in the past, hit him hard. Her scent still haunted him. Her taste… Thinking about the way they'd been together…

Blood rushed to his groin. He squirmed. His jeans suddenly felt too tight, forcing him to adjust them. Not an easy accomplishment while seated in his saddle.

"She's hard to define."

*"Almost as hard as your cock."*

"Leave my cock out of this."

*"Can't. It's very important to our plan if you want to survive and if you want to help her through the change."*

"I know. Just. Not yet."

There'd been a reason Bryan rode out here to meet her, but after seeing her, he hesitated. Something kept him from stepping forward. He wasn't ready to face her and explain.

*"A plan is what you need...and courage."*

Hunter was right. He'd have to think this through and gather the guts from somewhere because they couldn't wait much longer. "What a helluva mess." He scrubbed his hand over his face and frowned. "She didn't know there would be these kinds of consequences for loving me." Neither had he.

Correction, it wasn't loving him that caused this. It was declaring that love while making love that bound them.

They'd made the mistake of falling in love with each other, and when she claimed she loved him, without realizing what he was doing, he'd spoken the vows that unwittingly claimed her as his mate.

"There has to be a way to explain what I am. What she is. What she will become. What I did to her—"

*"Unintentionally."*

"True, but that's not going to make a difference. I have to convince her we can't live without each other. And I'm pretty damn sure she hates me."

*"Facing her, angry or not, is inevitable. You can't let your mate suffer. It's something your cat will fight."*

"I'd never let her go through what I did, not alone. Not if you and I can help her through her transition."

Bryan breathed a sigh of relief as he watched her gallop off in the opposite direction. He still had to face her and explain everything. She deserved to know why he'd left.

*"You going after her?"*

"Yeah. But not now." Bryan shook his head and looked up. "You follow her and keep an eye on her while I check the house…"

Hunter stood next to the rock, a man now, naked and muscular.

"What the hell?" Bryan spun around, glancing in all directions. "Why did you shift?"

"We have to go down there and look around. I

don't want to spook her horses. My cat would rile 'em up. They're not used to our scent the way our horses are."

"Well, for fuck's sake, put on some clothes before someone thinks we're playing Brokeback Mountain out here? These people know me."

Without commenting, Hunter whistled one short, sharp trill. An Appaloosa rounded the brush-covered ledge and trotted to him giving him a playful nudge.

"We're shifters and you're worried about someone thinking we're gay?" Hunter raised a sarcastic brow at Bryan and chuckled before he reached into the saddlebag and pulled out a set of clothes.

"The people around here are closed-minded. It almost would be easier to explain someone catching you shifting."

"I don't get why you're worried."

"People around here shoot first and consider the questions later."

"Then they'd shoot me either way, covered with mountain lion fur or naked man skin?"

"Yeah, either way you're not safe. So stay dressed or out of sight as a cat."

"Sure thing. Is there a back way to wherever she's heading?"

"You can track her from the ridge behind the ranch. It'll give you a clear view, and she won't spot you up there."

"You'll meet me out there later, then?"

While Hunter finished dressing, Bryan worried, mumbling, "Sure. How the hell can I explain?"

"Honestly."

"Really, Hunter? What if she turns me down?"

“It’s a chance you have to take, and we both know she isn’t going to have a choice sooner or later.”

“So, should I dump the whole thing on her and wait for her to laugh in my face before she calls 911 for the mentally deranged? You think that’s the way to go?”

“Show her. Don’t tell her.” Rising into the air with a swift, graceful move, Hunter mounted the horse bareback. After giving the Appaloosa a gentle pat, he started down the winding path toward the ranch. “You claim she’s tough. Then she’ll handle it.”

“Maybe you’re right.” Bryan followed. “I hate feeling like this…so uncertain. I’ve never stopped wanting her.”

“And you won’t. The need will only get stronger between the two of you.”

Bryan wasn’t sure that was possible. But until he could explain his disappearance, he figured he was in for the cold shoulder from the one woman he needed more than air. When they said good-bye, they expected he’d be back in five weeks, not five years.

His damn balls tightened and his cock pressed tighter against his zipper, remembering their last night together. The promises. How he’d loved her. How he’d infected her and bound her without realizing what he was doing.

Hell, he was damn certain Lacey wasn’t going to be anxious to relieve his needs any time soon. Not until she believed his story, as fantastic as it was. He had to convince her he’d stayed away for her own good, at least until he discovered she’d started developing symptoms.

“Sun’s not going to come to a halt in the sky and time’s a-wasting. You should do this before we see her at the reunion."

"Hell, I'm not completely sure I understand my reasons for leaving back then. After the attack I wasn't myself."

"Maybe it was some kind of subconscious awareness."

"But my reasons for not coming back before now—I understood them." Damn straight he understood. He'd justified every one of those reasons a million times. And they all boiled down to what he'd become, what he'd always been, and the lies he'd lived with.

"Why stall?"

"I don't know." He wasn't sure why he'd come out here, today. Was it too soon or too late?

"Why come here today and not confront her?"

"I'm keeping an eye on her, keeping her safe…"

"And?"

"Hiding out here was one way of seeing her without her seeing me—a way of gauging her reaction." Unfortunately, the reaction was the one he'd feared. Bryan hadn't missed the pained look on her face when she came out of the house or the anger in her stride as she stalked to the barn.

"She's hurtin'. Plain enough to see that on her face." Hunter stroked his horse's mane.

"I know." Bryan felt her emotions as if they were his own and had ever since the first time they'd made love to each other. He'd always been able to feel her moods when she was anywhere within his vicinity. Today was no different.

"Yeah. So what are you waiting for?"

"It doesn't bring me any satisfaction knowing I'm

hurtin' her again." Bryan's horse tripped then sidestepped a rock. Usually surefooted, the horse surprised him. Bryan sensed his rotten mood was affecting the animal. He gave him a few pats to relax him then finished his thought. "…or that I still have the power to do it."

"No, but it does mean she still cares. And you need that on your side."

By now, she'd received his message. He knew how much it hurt her, yet there was something else he sensed that concerned him more. She was seething angry. How was he going to get past that?

He groaned.

"What?"

"She's pissed."

"It's better for her to be angry than hurtin', Bryan. She'll get over anger. And you can't deal with the pain you bring her. It makes your lion crazy. Anger is better."

"I get that. But, Hunter, you know it's that internal strength that I love most about her."

"Let's go. You find out what you can at the house, and I'll watch after her 'til you get there."

"She's going to the planning meeting tomorrow. Thomas said the committee will head over to O'Malley's for happy hour."

"Good, you can catch her off guard with everyone all around, since she won't be expecting you until the next day."

"Look, Hunter, I'm not sure surprise is the best way to deal with Lacey."

"It's a public place. She'll be forced to be civil—"

"Maybe…" He doubted public surprise was the

best way to handle a dangerous five-year reunion. “I don’t know. The waves of anger rolling off her were significant. She wasn’t showing signs of civility returning anytime soon.”

## Chapter Six

When the final run through with the caterers hit a snag, Lacey stayed behind to smooth out the details. Thomas and the others agreed to hold a chair for her at O'Malley's.

Lacey's skin prickled the minute she'd walked through the door. She looked around the old bar and grille and didn't notice anything different except a sizzle in the air. Her skin tingled that way when she thought about Bryan. For a moment, she wondered if her rash was returning. She stood on her toes, looking for her friends, and tried to put Bryan out of her mind.

After reading his email, she was almost determined to skip the actual party. But as head of the planning committee, she wouldn't be able to play hooky tomorrow no matter how badly she wanted. It seemed safe joining everyone tonight, and she planned to set the stage for an early retreat tomorrow. There was no reason to stay once everything was underway. Maybe she'd have a convenient relapse of whatever it was she'd had these last few months. If she was lucky, she'd end up hospitalized again before the reunion party. Surely, a hospital stay was a sufficient excuse for bailing. Everyone would understand that.

Above a few heads in the crowd, she spotted Thomas's tall frame with his hand up, waving wildly at her from the other side of the bar.

After a quick internal evaluation, a relapse didn't look like it was likely to happen any time soon. Other than being frustrated and hot, she was actually feeling stronger tonight than she had the last few months…if she ignored her lousy mental attitude. She attributed the blame for that to Bryan, but she couldn't remember the last time she'd had this much pent up energy. Maybe the anger strengthened her resolve.

Smiling and greeting her way past a few old friends, Lacey forced herself to block all thoughts about Bryan and to focus on the jubilee.

Several of the town regulars played pool in the back, early arrivals were renewing old acquaintances, and O'Malley looked pleased as a proud poppa with the turn out. Tonight was a precursor to tomorrow's more formal events at the country club. This evening, the old man was reaping the rewards of maintaining the local watering hole for over thirty years. Young and old remembered downing their first legal beer at this bar. After the jubilee parade and the town festivities, everyone would end up back here tomorrow night.

Lacey turned to Thomas, who was getting desperate for her attention and had started shouting her name above the music.

"Be right there," she yelled back. Squeezing between the tables, she headed to the bar and her friends.

"Hey, great turn out," she said when Thomas stood.

"Yup. Plenty of alumni to brain pick." He winked and offered her the seat between Keiran and Donna before he walked up to a few guys she didn't recognize and began talking.

"Thanks for saving me a seat. I don't think my feet

could hold up for five minutes more."

"No problem." Keiran handed her a mug and poured her a beer.

The four of them had spent every free minute for the past two months hashing out the jubilee details. Earlier, they finished the last of the plans and intended to wind down with a few beers and wings.

"Did you order?"

"Yeah. Thomas is drinking bottled. We ordered a pitcher and wings. They should be out soon. Figured you'd missed lunch as usual," Donna said. "You've been too busy working on the jubilee to eat properly, girl."

The idea of tomorrow sent a chill up Lacey's spine and her stomach turned to lead. "I'm sure Keiran and Thomas filled you in on my medical issues. I haven't had much of an appetite."

Donna smiled. "No secrets between us. Hope Doc has an answer soon. You look good."

Thomas returned. "She does look better… Mmmm, in fact, you look incredible." He released a low hiss when he bent in to kiss her hello.

She brushed off the compliment. "Get serious, Thomas."

He might be the hottest-looking cowboy around, but she knew his secret passion. He wasn't playing solely for the home team. He made no secret anymore about swinging both ways. A nice cowgirl with a pretty cowboy accessory was his preference. A ménage was always more to his liking than vanilla sex with either. As far as Lacey was concerned, for those and so many other reasons, he was not her first choice for dating material.

He ignored her rebuff and wrapped his arm around her shoulder.

"Donna, everything all set for the parade tomorrow?" Lacey asked.

"Yup, everything's set to go off as planned thanks to you. Now, if only I can just find something…or someone…interesting to do tonight." Donna Barton owned the spa, the bookstore, and the bridal shop. At thirty, she was single, sexy, and too smart for her own good. Lacey watched her roll her eyes to her left. The brawny-looking cowboy, in jeans and a shirt wrapped so tightly across his chest Lacey worried he'd pop his snaps, did a quick turn in Donna's direction. He whipped around to the flashy redhead, looked her Barbie doll body up and down, and gave her a slow smile and an interested grin.

So much for Donna's company for the rest of the evening, Lacey thought and turned to her other team member. "Keiran? How's the country club?"

"Ready! Luv ya, Lace, but I'm done, and more than ready to put my feet up." Keiran blushed. Putting her feet up was their euphemism for getting it on. From the number of times Lacey heard Keiran mention she was putting her feet up lately, she and Jack must be fucking like bunnies.

"I'm only hanging with you guys until Jack gets off work." She looked at her phone when it vibrated with the text message. "The tests say tonight is right," she whispered. "Oh, that's him now. He's coming by to pick me up."

"I guess that leaves you with me." Thomas smiled at Lacey and wiggled his eyebrows suggestively at her.

"Yeah, so what's new?"

His gaze dropped to her breasts when she reached for the pitcher next to him. “That dress for starters.”

She followed his stare, shook her head, and glared at him while she poured beer in her mug. “What the hell’s the matter with you?”

“What? I like that dress.”

He let out a low moan when she took a deep breath.

“Since when did you suddenly become a breast man?”

“I’m not. I’m an ass man. I like your ass, too. What’s wrong with appreciating it all?” He whispered, “Besides, I seldom get to play with tits as pretty as yours.”

“Humph. Men. You are so easily distracted with sex.”

“There’s something to be said for sex. You should try it sometime. Now, really, what are these for?” He reached out with the side of his fingers and lightly touched the tassels holding the bodice of her dress together.

“Oh. Uhh, I guess decoration.”

He shook his head once, tilted the bottle in his hand to her breasts, and raised his brows. “Those don’t need any decoratin’, hon.” He took a long swig from the beer, never taking his eyes off her. “They’re puurrfect.”

His unabashed interest in her cleavage almost made her laugh. “Really, Thomas, I don’t know how to respond.”

“If I tug on these, what happens to this dress?” His fingers teased at the tassels.

“Don’t even think about it.” Lacey narrowed her eyes at him and grinned. “Are you comin’ on to me?”

"What if I am?"

Tonight the pain made her think about drowning in sex and putting everything else out of her mind. Thomas would be up to the challenge. He shouldn't tempt her like this. "Don't."

"Why not?" he asked.

"I'd say, you better be careful. Watch out if you're not serious. Tonight, I just might take you up on the offer and try to lure you away from your usual fare."

"You wouldn't have to try to lure me. I've been waiting forever for you to succumb to my charms. Besides, I don't have a usual fare. You know me. I have no preference as long as the fare's hot and sassy."

"I'm serious—"

"I'm never serious. So what? But I'm serious where you're concerned, my friend."

"Hate to interrupt your rotten attempt at seduction, Tommy…" Keiran rolled her eyes at Thomas and handed Lacy her beer. "Here, you might need this if you even consider his offer. Jack is here. I'm heading home."

"Why do you insist on calling me by my elementary school nickname?" Thomas huffed. "It's so childish."

"Sorry, Tom—Thomas. Old habits and all… I'll leave you two to your own vices."

"Thanks, I'll have you know I have no vices." Lacey laughed. "I've spent years cleaning up my act."

"Gotta go." Keiran wriggled her fingers in a good-bye wave. "Good night, kiddies. You, too, Donna. See ya tomorrow."

Donna waved over her shoulder but kept her attention focused on the cowboy.

"Well, back to vices. I have enough for both of us," Thomas announced.

"Well, now everyone knows that."

He really was handsome and sexy. Cupping her chin with his cool hands, he turned her face and tilted it so she had to look up to stare him in the eyes. He was close enough that she could feel his breath on her lips.

"You're playin' with fire," she reminded him.

"Hmm, fire? Jalapeño hot?" He pecked her on the lips playfully and fanned his lips. "Mmm. Hot!"

She chuckled. There was no way to stay annoyed with him. "Yes. Extra spicy jalapeno."

"You know I prefer my fare extra spicy and would never turn away from a little variety, hon. Especially, if you're on the menu."

"You are flirty tonight." She pecked him back on the lips and laughed.

"Hey, I have a few friends who'd like some hot ménage action." He shifted his eyes in the direction of the men he'd spoken to earlier. "We could both get lucky." His laugh was low and naughty.

Lacey choked on the beer from the mug she'd put to her lips. Her face flushed while she tried to catch her breath.

When she did, she spit out a sound of disgust. Then, suddenly, the picture of two men making love to her set her insides all aflutter. Not that she would ever consider doing anything like that, let alone with her best friend. She looked at him and memories of them hunting grasshoppers washed through her mind.

She giggled. *No. Never Thomas.* She loved him…but not like that. "Eww!"

"I think it's exactly what you need, and I'd be

honored to introduce you to the steamier side of erotic lovemaking, especially if I get a crack at the dark haired guy, too."

"Oh, how my heart is all aflutter with your generous offer. But darlin', I'm not ready to be your wingman." She glared at him and punched his arm playfully. "You're my friend, Thomas. Sex with you would be…just…gross."

His handsome smile disappeared. "Oh, thanks for stomping all over my ego."

"Don't look at me like that. You know what I mean."

"You're one of the few women who's ever really interested me."

"Really? Liar. I've heard too many stories about your conquests. All of them. I'm not flattered. Even if it was the truth, I know why you want me. I'm one of the few who can resist you. I've seen you in diapers."

"And out of them. There's more to me now." He ran a hand around her waist and bent to kiss her neck. His hard cock pressed against her thigh when he kissed his way to her ear. "See. And I like your firm, round ass, hon. I've always dreamed about taking you there while some stud pounds into mine."

"Oh, my God, Thomas. Too. Much. Information!" She inhaled and swallowed. The thought was so outrageous she couldn't even think of a comment.

"Are you blushing, Lacey? I didn't think there was anything I could say anymore that could make you blush. Uh, unless… Are you thinking about it?" He released a loud snort. "Tell me you are."

"Hush!" Her cheeks were hot. "I am not thinking about it. Why are you doing this to me tonight?"

They'd been close all their lives. He'd always been there for her and for Bryan. Tonight Thomas's behavior was way out of character.

"Why can't we be BFWB?"

"What?"

"Best friends with benefits! Everyone's doing it."

"Not us. I want to stay best friends."

"Tomorrow is the reunion. You going with anyone?"

"N–no…" What was he getting at?

"He'll be there… I saw his name on the list." Thomas lifted his beer and turned away from her. "Are you going to be all right?"

"Is that what this is all about? Oh, please tell me you're not offering me a pity fuck, Thomas."

"Pity?" He had the audacity to laugh in her face. "Dance with me, Lacey." He shook his head and pressed his finger to her lips when she started to object. "Humor me and shush."

He pulled her off the barstool, took her glass out of her hand, and put it on the bar. "Keep your eye on our drinks, Donna."

She nodded, still not turning her attention away from the cowboy with the tight shirt and biceps to die for. Before Lacey knew where she was heading, she and Thomas were moving through the tight-knit crowd toward the back of the dance floor.

He hauled her into his embrace and whispered, "Watch the guys who are hanging around back here, and then ask me that question again." He cocked a brow in the direction of a few ranch hands she recognized. A couple of them had tried to get her attention when she came into town for supplies. Billy Trenton had even ridden out to the ranch, making an excuse to see her over some old tires he heard she was looking at for her tractor. Sure, she was aware several of the guys were interested, but they'd been easy enough to refuse.

Thomas put his hands on her hips and walked her out to the middle of the dance floor, leaned into her ear, and said, "There's not a male breathing who would consider you a pity fuck. Trust me. I'm about to prove it to you."

"You're gay—"

"Correction. Bi. I know what I am and you should be flattered it's never prevented my dick from getting hard around you."

"I'm not flattered. You should be more discriminating."

"I'd jump at the chance to bury myself inside your ass while some nice cowboy rides your pussy." He pulled her tighter to him, and rubbed himself against her mound to prove it. "Or vice versa. I like to be fucked while I'm fucking. So sue me."

"Slut," she whispered as he swung her out of his embrace.

Thomas opened his mouth wide, threw his head back, and laughed. "So true, hon. So true."

Then he enfolded her in his arms and two-stepped her around the dance floor to the music, swinging her out so hard her skirt flew high, wrapping around her hips. And she wondered how much ass cheek she'd flashed. Her T-backs wouldn't hide much.

Before long, Lacey's curiosity got the better of her and she did as he suggested. The men standing around had stopped what they were doing to watch. Some adjusted jeans. Some stuck a hand in a pocket—some stuck both hands in their pockets to make more room for the bulges. She noticed the narrowed eyes, an occasional pull on their drinks, and long, hard swallows. They kept their eyes glued to her until the music paused.

"Thanks," she said when Thomas pulled her back against his large frame. "I feel better."

"So are we good for later?"

"Hell, no." Lacey giggled.

"No? I'm devastated."

"Not gonna happen. Ever! I'm fine with tomorrow." She hesitated. "I'll handle it."

The parade would be fun and the jubilee wasn't bothering her. Seeing the out-of-towners back after so long would be a treat. Honestly, she was okay with everything except for one thing—Bryan.

She had to unclench her teeth thinking about the way he announced he was alive and well. Truth be told, what really riled her was the way he'd done it. An email. Did the bastard think he could email her out of the blue and make everything better with a few mundane words?

The concept made Lacey fume every time she thought about it.

"A penny for your thoughts."

"Trust me. You don't want to know." Lacey picked up the thread of their conversation and blew him an air kiss. "And…I don't think you'll need my help getting lucky in this crowd."

Thomas gave her that notorious sexy smile, complete with his teasing wink, and tugged a little on her tassels. "Okay, I have to admit you're right, but I still really want to pull your strings."

## Chapter Seven

Five minutes before Lacey walked in and sat down at the bar with Thomas, Bryan made Hunter move quietly to the back of the room. They kept their hats on, concealing a part of their faces. Everyone would still recognize him, and Bryan didn't want to draw attention to himself before tomorrow.

"You know"—Hunter faced Bryan and warned him—"one day she's going to ask why you didn't come for her sooner."

"I know, dammit. If I knew about her father I would have. Thomas should have told me about that and her symptoms sooner. Why would he keep that from me?"

Hunter shrugged. "No need to start second-guessing his motives now, for God's sake. We just have to find a way to convince her you didn't know what happened."

Bryan released a sardonic laugh. "Yeah, and that I didn't have anything to do with her father's death. I can't help thinking she suspects it may have been me. Hell, she knew about my blackouts back then."

"Don't worry. We'll find out what happened to her father and clear you."

They remained in the shadows, watching as Thomas teased Lacey. Every second Bryan spent watching the man touch her was pure torture. Being in the same room with her scent and being this close was different from watching her at a distance.

When the skirt whipped around her tan thighs, tight from riding her horses daily, he knew every man in the bar wished he could be the one she rode home. Bryan's chest rumbled with the lion's low growl. The skirt fanned her scent out through the room, making his cock press hard against his zipper. She always was unaware of the effect she had on men, but Bryan knew Thomas wasn't. He wanted to rip out his friend's heart and claw out every man's eyes who watched her dance.

"What the hell is wrong with him? Flaunting her like that?"

"You know that guy?"

"Yeah, I know him. That's Thomas. Our contact. My friend. But friend or not, he needs to take his hands off her."

If she'd been in his arms, Bryan would have kept her wrapped up close, tight against his body, in the shadows, protected from the other men's gazes. He'd have made a statement, a claim.

But Thomas couldn't do that—no one else could. Lacey belonged to him. Bryan smiled then frowned. He had already staked that claim. She would never be free from their bond, whether she wanted to be or not.

"Strange. It almost looks like he's playing her to an audience." Hunter sounded reasonable and calm.

"He needs to cover her up."

"Calm down, Bryan. He saw us standing in the corner earlier. Gave me a pretty thorough going over. If you get what I mean?"

"Thomas was checking you out?"

"Yeah, I thought he was. Then she walked in and

now he's all over her."

"There's something different about him." Bryan rubbed a hand over his chin. "Guy couldn't keep the chicks off him. Dated around, never any particular girl for long. He's always been into the kinky stuff."

"Well, he wants her. That's obvious."

"Always did. But he never acted on it with her. He and Lacey have been friends since they were in diapers. He'd do anything for her, or she for him, but she was never interested in him…that way."

"He eyeballed me, and recognized us, so he knows we're here, and he's flirting with her. What does that tell you?"

"He has a death wish."

"No. Guess again."

"Before Lacey and I were an item, he wanted me to do a girl from Amarillo with him. The date never panned out, and then I started dating Lacey. He never brought it up again. He was a friend, a good friend to both of us. Helped us out, got her home safely when I couldn't risk us getting caught together. I didn't want my son-of-a-bitch father to take it out on her dad."

Just then something Thomas said made Lacey laugh. A few minutes later, she blushed and giggled. Bryan's throat constricted. He used to be able to make her react that way. It saddened him that someone else was the one making her smile now and he was the one causing her pain.

"He's still her friend—still doing whatever it takes to make her happy," Bryan said.

"Can't fault him for that."

"Friend or not, part of him wants her. I can taste it in the air." Bryan growled beneath his breath.

"Yeah, so can I. But you need to stay in control, bro."

"He's making me jealous."

"Yeah, he is." It didn't take much for Hunter to fill in the blanks.

"Damn him. I guess I wasn't specific enough when I called him and asked for his help." Bryan wanted to break Thomas's fingers and wipe the smile off his too-perfect face. He cursed again. "I know what he's doing."

"Bro, think about it. He's doing this on purpose. Teasing you. He's forcing your hand."

"Maybe I'll thank him for it, someday." A frown furrowed Bryan's brow, and he spoke softly, almost to himself. "Right now, if he doesn't back off and take his hands off her, my lion is urging me to rip his throat out."

"There's only one way to get his hands off her without violence."

"How?"

"Dance with her."

Hunter had a point. Bryan took off his hat and put it down on the table as he stood. His throat tightened when he stepped out of the shadows into the light. Lacey's eyes flickered in his direction and held him in place. Heads turned. Pool balls stopped hitting each other, and several shocked gasps filled the silence in the room. The fast music segued from one song to the next. An appropriate somebody-done-somebody-wrong song started just as Bryan's gaze locked with Lacey's.

He moved cautiously toward her. Everyone quieted as he reached a hand out to her and she absently lifted hers in response.

The same spark she felt the first time she saw him sizzled across the room, mesmerizing her now as it had then. When their eyes met that first moment after she was bound to him, her essence locked with his, shackled by a mere glance.

She wondered if she'd ever seen anything more beautiful than those eyes. They'd once sparkled with life and laughter, energy and joy—hope and love. Now they were fixed on her, almost beseeching her. Her stomach flipped.

He stood in front of her with his hand extended and a look on his face that said his heart was in his hand—take it or reject it.

Lacey swore the world narrowed to a corridor linking the two of them when he stepped closer to take her hand in his. She involuntarily lifted it. Their fingertips touched, but no more.

"Dance with me, Lacey." His voice was a little deeper than she remembered. It sounded thick with emotion and need. His eyes searched her face with guarded interest, looking for something she wouldn't show him.

His simple plea asked too much.

The choice was hers. She didn't react.

The blood running through her veins turned warmer than it had been in years. All this time she swore her heart pumped pure ice water after he left. Ice was hard, impenetrable. It would take more than Bryan showing up for a dance to melt her frozen heart.

Then he stepped closer. The scent he carried was the same. Bryan. Sweet, fresh air and woods. She inhaled to savor the moment, and then he whispered the silly rhyme he'd made up that first time.

“Won’t you dance with me, Lacey? Take a chance with me?” His hand slid into hers lightly.

He remembered.

Something inside her shifted. The ice around her heart cracked at his touch. The trickle she felt was the warm blood seeping from her shattered heart. Pain sliced through her. The same pain as when a limb falls asleep and wakes up. You know the pins and needles are coming and dread it, but it’s inevitable. There was no alternative. She had to experience the bleeding heart like a stab wound.

Damn him.

He was in her personal space and hurting her with memories, killing her with his words and his scent. She did the only thing she could think of to protect herself and to prevent him from following when she ran.

She attacked.

****

Bryan tried to breathe without throwing up as he unrolled from the fetal position. He still had one hand cupped to his groin and the other to his jaw.

“Man. she’s really mad at you,” Thomas said, glancing back as Lacey disappeared through the front door.

“Hey bro, I’m sorry,” Hunter said, as he helped his brother up off the floor.

There was a glint of humor in his voice. Bryan didn’t think he sounded very sorry, at all. Though, he couldn’t speak to make that observation, so he scowled as his brother chuckled. His jaw was still locked from the roundhouse blow he’d taken from Lacey after she kneed him in the groin.

“How was I to know she’d go for your balls and

then punch you in the face?"

Bryan gagged a couple of times on the way up off the floor, clutching Hunter on one side and Thomas on the other.

"Shit, she's quick. I didn't see that coming," Bryan wheezed.

"Hey, sorry about your…" Thomas cleared his throat. "Uhm, your balls okay?"

Bryan groaned, standing hunched over. "Got ice?"

"You going to ice your balls here?" Thomas asked.

"No, you dumb fuck, it's for my jaw." Bryan cursed at his friend with his hands still on his knees. He tried to take a deep breath.

"Right. Here, let me help."

Hunter helped him back to their table. "Your balls okay, bro?"

"I'm not sure."

A few minutes later, Thomas handed him the ice-filled bar towel. With one hand holding the ice to his jaw, Bryan extended his hand to Thomas. "Sorry I snapped at you."

"No problem. It's good to see you, Bryan. You should probably go somewhere you can ice those balls, too."

"Suddenly everyone's interested in my balls. She shoves them halfway up my throat, and the two of you can't stop askin' after 'em."

Thomas smiled. "I figured she'd be inclined to take better care with them."

"Where is she?"

"She ran."

Hunter put Bryan's hat on his head and said, "By the way she flashed out of here, like someone set her on fire, I gather she's not quite ready to deal with you."

"Ready or not, she's going to have to deal with me."

"She's been feeling poorly, lately." Thomas put a restraining hand on Bryan's arm, but dropped it when Bryan snarled. "Hey, just give her some time."

"She's had five years. Time's up."

Bryan left her because he wanted to save her from what he was. Walking away… No, running away without a word had almost killed him. Now he was back because he had infected her. She was running out of time, and time was something they didn't have. Her change was imminent. After touching her, he was more certain than ever. Her body temperature was rising. The change was on her already.

"I don't know how I'm going to get her to listen. If looks could kill, she would've done me in when I walked up to her. Hell, I only asked her to dance. What's she going to do when I tell her she has to marry me?"

"Marry you?" Thomas laughed and gave Bryan a wry smile. "That may take some fast talkin'. Let me give you some advice. I'd suggest when the time comes, you 'ask' her—don't think to 'tell' her anything."

"She doesn't know what's good for her."

"Well, I'd say she made her feelings pretty damn clear about what she doesn't think is good for her."

"Right. Anything to do with me."

Hunter slapped Bryan on the shoulder while he and Thomas laughed it up at his expense.

"She is still Lacey, and she has a million reasons to be angry, Bryan. Your dad was an ass to her when you disappeared. If not that, then she certainly has cause about her father's killing. I guess you showin' up took her off guard. She's hurtin'."

"I'll find out what happened to her father, I swear."

"We better do some checking. Early tomorrow we'll start with old man Cauldwell." Hunter added, low enough so Thomas couldn't hear, "Full moon's coming soon, Bryan. There's not much time left to convince her."

"Your father's out of town until tomorrow," Thomas said. "Your brother is out at the ranch keeping an eye on things until he gets back. Tory may have more answers than your old man."

"Then we better work fast. We can pressure Tory and the men before he gets back." Bryan brushed himself off and took his beer off the table. "Thanks, Thomas. I'll check back with you later and let you know how things went with Lacey."

"You know where she's going? Right?"

"Yeah. I know where she's headed and why." He emptied the drink. "I'll give her a little time to cool off before I go after her."

# Chapter Eight

Lacey picked up her rifle when she heard the horses acknowledge each other at the mouth of the cave. The crunch of boots on leaves and gravel sounded familiar, but there were two of them.

She knew Bryan would come. The surprise was that he'd waited so long.

Smart man. She'd been mad enough to have shot him if he'd shown up sooner. He'd figured out that much. Or maybe it took him all this time to retrieve his balls.

Without turning around, she released the breath she'd been holding and sighed. He stepped into the dim light at the mouth of the cave.

"You a glutton for punishment, Bryan?" She put the rifle against the wall so as not to be tempted and refused to look at him. "What are you doing here?"

"I'm here for the reunion. I emailed you—"

"Yeah, got it, *old friend*," Lacey snapped.

"Then you know why I'm here."

She inhaled and turned, glaring at him with all the anger she could muster. Meeting his earnest, golden eyes leached the air from her lungs. Being near him never failed to turn her into a quivering mound of sexual need. Lust warred with anger and pain, and dammit…hope.

"You know what I mean. Don't act dense," she

snarled between tight lips and ground her teeth. “Why are you here? At the grotto?”

At our place, she added to herself. She wanted to turn away before the sting of seeing him so close overwhelmed her, but she couldn’t. Only a full-frontal confrontation would do.

He didn’t answer or move. Instead, he shifted his attention, examined the walls, and searched until his glance touched the spot where their initials were carved in the rock wall inside a heart. Then, he turned to her.

“Why are you?” he asked. His hard gaze softened.

His ability to remain as still as the stone around them always disconcerted her.

“I asked first.”

“Maybe I wanted to revisit old times.” His quiet voice, even deeper than it had earlier, was mellower when he asked, “You, too?”

“No.” She snapped out the lie. “I’m over old times, old friend.”

“You came here yesterday, last night, and the night before—”

“You followed me? Watched me?” That’s why she thought about him before the email. She sensed him. “How dare—”

“It’s dangerous for you out here alone.” His eyes flashed golden flecks at her.

“Really? I’m touched by your concern. I’ve been coming out here alone for…” She stopped speaking. Damn him. She hadn’t intended to tell him that. Did he care? Had there been anyone else?

“You were the only one I ever came here with, Lacey.”

He answered as if she’d asked.

He'd grown into a powerful-looking man with a wide jaw, thick sinewy arms, and broad shoulders. The boy had filled out his tall, youthful frame with slabs of lean, heavy muscle. He'd become a man and, if possible, his presence affected her even more now than it had.

Yet behind the man's eyes were the younger ones. The eyes of the boy she'd once loved with her entire being. Her heart opened after his hand touched hers, and the ice melted. Now her heart cried crimson tears of blood. Disregarding how he made her feel wasn't going to be easy. Not when every emotion possible streaked through her, shattering her defenses. She closed her eyes and prayed for strength because, God help her, she wanted answers.

Where have you been? What have you been doing? Why didn't you come back to me?

Too proud, she wouldn't ask them. If he didn't offer her answers, she'd bite off her tongue before she brought up the past. One question. She would risk one question.

"Why now?"

He moved with the grace of a large cat, raised his hand, placed it over their initials in the carving, and kept it there when he shrugged. "I discovered there is no turning back. It was time."

It was time? Not the answer she expected. Anger returned, thank goodness. She shook her head. "It took you all these years to think about home, old times, old friends? Me?" she asked, the emphasis on his words.

The question tasted bitter on her tongue and more bitter in her heart. When she stared into his unblinking eyes looking for the truth, the only sign he gave that she'd made a direct hit was when his jaw clenched before he answered.

This time his words were an erotic whisper. "No, Lacey. Not a minute's gone by without me thinking about you—us."

She was about to give him credit for reining in his emotions when his eyes narrowed, taking her all in with a hunger she sensed to her core. Then his tone changed.

"I didn't give a damn...don't give a damn about anything else, but I did and still do about you." His controlled pitch was a low growl.

At one time, their love had been so new, so bright, and beautiful—like a raging fire in the night. When it blinked out, the light disappeared. The dark dull contrast had been almost too much to bear. She squeezed her eyes shut, keeping hope out—unable to risk more pain. No, no—not again. The threads holding her together turned into ropes reaching out to him. The knot in her throat prevented her from screaming.

"I'm sorry, Lacey. I don't know where to start. I didn't know about your father—"

"Don't," her voice crackled like shattered glass, and her throat felt like she'd swallowed it. Holding her hand up to keep him from taking the step toward her, she stepped back.

"Lacey. You didn't think... Tell me you don't think I had anything to do with his death."

She turned away, afraid he'd see the truth in her eyes. "You admitted the blackouts, told me about having blood on your hands. You disappeared. Within days, they found my father dead." Mauled. "What do you expect me to think?"

"I'd never..." Bryan's expression filled with

horror. "I loved your father. He was more father to me than Cauldwell ever was."

Her resolve wavered. "I didn't believe you'd hurt him, but then, I never thought you would hurt me the way you did, either."

He reached out, but she shook her head and recoiled. If he touched her, she'd dissolve, splinter, crumble. "You don't owe me any explanations. We were kids. I just…"

No matter what, she believed his family always knew what happened to him because there were rumors of a falling out between the old man and Bryan the morning he left. Then nothing.

"You just what?"

"Nothing. Apparently, I didn't know you as well as I thought."

"…just what?" he repeated.

"I just wondered," she said, finally finishing her sentence but not her thoughts. *I just…thought you were dead. Died myself a little when you didn't show up.*

Bryan heard the way she cut off her words and pulled back her emotions. The rest, his cat's instincts heard with his mind even without her speaking.

Not touching her as the pain gathered behind her eyes was the hardest thing he ever did…with the exception of leaving her in the first place. Pain radiated off her and through him—the old pain he caused when he'd left her and this new raw pain his presence caused.

She wouldn't admit how much he'd hurt her, but he suddenly understood. Being apart from her mate had hurt her as much as it had him. How would he ever make this up to her?

"You have to know if there was a way to return for

you, I would have."

"No. I didn't know that. I was twenty, insecure..." Her eyes iced over and her quiet response stabbed right through him. "Your family was powerful. Your father and brother hated me because... I don't know why. Maybe because I was the foreman's daughter? Someone a Cauldwell slept with, not someone they married."

"Don't say that." Bryan never cared. "I didn't pay attention to what my family thought. I asked you, didn't I? I planned to marry—"

"You didn't come back!"

Bryan's heart clenched. She sounded broken. "I wanted to."

"What's the real story, Bryan?"

His mother died when he was five and his father remarried. After Tory was born, Bryan was treated like an outcast. His father left him alone as long as he didn't do anything to embarrass the impeccable family name. Bryan never belonged.

"Answer me, dammit. Was it amnesia? Just get out of prison or something?" Lacey leaned in and poked him in the chest for emphasis. "What keeps someone away for five years? Oh, yeah and let me add this...without a phone call, an email, or an effing card?" The finger dug in with each word, branding her fury on his chest.

He wanted to fold her in his arms but the anger rippling off her warned him to stay put. "I promise I'll explain."

Accepting and acclimating to who and what he was, then surviving in a world new to him had been a huge adjustment. He almost went mad when Hunter told him he had probably infected her the last time they were together. But when Hunter checked with Thomas, he said she was fine. So Bryan stayed away. In fact, he never intended to come back and put her through what he endured.

"If I had a choice, it would have been forever."

Her gaze snapped to his and her eyes flashed with fire. "Don't think you're doing me any favors showing up now." Her hands went to her hips and her anger overflowed, hitting him like a physical slap. "Go away, Bryan. I was doing just fine without you."

"Lacey, I didn't mean it like—"

"Look, I don't want or need any explanations."

"Yes, you do." He took a step toward her.

Her eyes flashed the warning and both her hands went up in defense when he tried to take a second step in her direction.

"Don't!" Lacey said, and her eyes blinked, shining with tears and something else.

He didn't dare set off too much anger and risk her change coming on before they prepared her. He raised his hands and took a step back. She was too angry to approach.

"You left m–me." Her voice cracked.

"I didn't want you involved with my kind of life—"

"You made that pretty clear."

"I meant problems."

Lacey raised one eyebrow, waiting for him to finish. This wasn't going well.

"I meant to say '…with everything that was going wrong.' I told you about the blackouts. Lacey, I didn't want you hurt."

"I was." Her chest rapidly rose and fell with each breath as she glared daggers at him—her body vibrating. "And I was alone after my father was killed…"

"I'm sorry. I thought I was doing what was best for you. I saw no other way…at the time."

"Enough." Lacey sighed, a tired, defeated sound. "Five years is a long time. Your reasons for not returning are your own. Mine, for not wanting to rehash old history, are personal. Let's forget it."

"I can't. I have to explain, and you have to listen carefully."

"I–I don't have to do anything." Her jaw clenched, and the pulse at her throat picked up pace. She released a low rumble of anger and growled, "You are so damned infuriating!"

She turned away, gathering her hair off her neck, rewound the thick blonde length into a bun, and clipped it up. In the time it took to accomplish the action, she collected herself and Bryan took the opportunity to admire her long, slim neck as she released another deep sigh. When she turned back to face him, she appeared composed.

"Look, let's drop the past. Tell me how you've been," she said.

"Sit down and I'll show you."

"I don't want to sit—"

"Lacey, please. Just sit. Nothing I tell you will mean as much as a demonstration. You need to see something."

"Hmmph." She grunted before she complied. Picking a large boulder in the corner, she plopped down, crossing her arms across her chest and frowned.

Good. When Hunter came in she needed to be far enough away from the entrance so she couldn't bolt, or they'd be chasing her down to explain.

"Hunter, come in."

## Chapter Nine

The huge mountain lion blocked the cave's entrance.

"Oh no, Bryan. Back up," Lacey shouted and jumped up.

He held up his hand to stop her. "Sit down and don't move," he warned.

Hunter wouldn't purposely hurt her, but if she ran, his instincts might take over. Bryan trusted him to perform the initial demonstration more than he trusted himself. Hunter spent a lifetime controlling his instincts. Bryan had only five short years.

"He won't hurt you. Just stay calm."

"Calm?" She stilled and lowered her voice, but her words sounded tense. "You're standing beside a large, male mountain lion. You do know that, right?"

"Yup. This is what kept me away from you and why I'm back."

Lacey turned and stared at him. He swore she hadn't taken a breath. "Sit down and keep breathing, Lacey."

"Right. Breathe," she muttered.

Bryan lowered his voice to match hers. "I've loved you all along."

When she sat down, her tentative gaze darted to the entrance where the big cat stood. Hunter dropped to the ground and lazed in the fading light at the mouth of the cave. His position guaranteed Lacey couldn't escape before Bryan had a chance to explain his predicament.

"There are things you don't know about me—things I didn't know about myself until I left."

Lacey started to move and protest, just as Hunter shook his huge head. She shut up and sat back down on her rock with a frown furrowing her brow.

"I was adopted."

"So?" Her eyes flicked to the lion and back to Bryan as she shrugged. "What's that got to do with…him?"

"He's my brother."

She snorted. "Better him than Tory."

She'd misunderstood—thought he meant "brother," like "buddy." Not the literal meaning. It made him want to pick her up and kiss her, but she kept shifting her attention between the large cat and his face. Worried. Bryan couldn't help the slight smile testing his mouth. He'd always loved her sarcasm, and he agreed with her about his brother. Tory was cruel. She had a thousand and one reasons to hate him and the whole family.

"You're right. He is an ass."

"If you say so." Her gaze darted to Hunter and back to him. She kept her voice steady as she spoke. "As far as I'm concerned, a pack of rats would be better relations than yours. If you're not a blood relation to old man Cauldwell, that's a plus in my book."

"Yeah, that was the upside to finding out about my background." She was right. Not being related to any of the Cauldwells could be considered a real plus. "It's not the whole story, though."

"I'm sorry if it bothers you, but plenty of people find out they're adopted and learn to deal with it."

"Some things take more adjusting to. That's what I've been doing, learning to deal with it. Do you mind if I come a little closer?"

"No. But is this the time to be discussing this?" Her expression darted to the lion and back to Bryan's face.

"It's okay. Hunter is going to show you why I left and didn't come ba—"

"I told you..." She looked confused. "It's not necessary to expla—"

"Yes, it is." He pressed a finger to her lips and placed a hand on her shoulder and said, "Hunter?"

The cat got up and shook, turned his back to them, and shimmered into his human form. His body was in shadows as the last light of the day backlit the cave entrance.

Lacey's hands gripped Bryan's shirt like a lifeline. Her eyes were as big as saucers in her pale face, and her mouth hung open, as if she wanted to say something but couldn't quite wrap her mind around the words.

He knew what a shock this was. She trembled beneath his hand. "Are you going to be all right?"

She nodded her head "yes." Then slowly, she shook it several times for "no." Confused, she closed her mouth before stammering out, "I–I don't know."

Hunter walked outside to put on his pants and returned a few minutes later with the rest of his clothes. "Nice to meet you, Lacey. I'm Hunter Harris, and I'm a shape-shifter, like Bryan here." He held out a hand.

Obviously shocked, she took his hand out of sheer good manners, but leaned around Hunter to look behind him like the lion was hiding there.

Her gaze kept pivoting between the two men while Hunter finished dressing. "No, it's not possible." Her mouth opened and the words spilled out.

Bryan expected that reaction. Maybe it was a good thing he'd held onto her elbow, because he felt her trembling kick up a notch before her knees buckled. Shock. He hoped she didn't collapse before they were finished. Believing she was made of sturdier stock than most was the only reason he agreed to do it this way.

"Lacey, take deep breaths and blow them out."

She let a small sigh escape.

"All the way. More. You need to sit down." He helped her back to the boulder. Although no amount of explaining would help, at the moment, he thought some sort of explanation was worth a shot.

"Honey, I know it's a shock. It was for me, too, but Hunter is teaching me how to deal with my natural instincts. He's helping me adjust."

"It's not a trick? Y–you do that, too?"

He cupped her face in his hands and looked straight into her eyes. "Yes, but I thought he'd be the best one to help me demonstrate."

"How?"

"…ability. I want to prove what I am to you. I need you to believe I wouldn't have left you without a damn good reason."

He reinforced his next words by gripping her shoulders. "Stay where you are. I don't have Hunter's control yet. He's here to protect you."

"Against what?"

"Not what. Me."

"You'd never—"

"I know what you think. I'd never hurt you. Not intentionally. But my lion doesn't know his own strength, and I can't risk a lapse that would put you in jeopardy. Trust Hunter and do as he says."

She nodded with her eyes darting left to right. "O–okay, but I still can't believe this."

"You will," he warned.

****

Bryan stepped back to the cave entrance and began removing his clothes, starting with his boots.

As he began to unbutton his shirt, Lacey's mouth went dry remembering his ripped abs and the way his skin felt when it rippled beneath her fingers.

He pulled the shirt out of his jeans, shrugging out of it like a practiced stripper. God, he looked good—beefier than before. What was previously a six pack was now an eight pack. And where his sides V'd into his hips… Hell, she could imagine holding onto those lats like handle bars while he fucked her.

She smelled the intoxicating scent lingering from his touch and cringed when her nipples tightened. Heat blasted through her, spreading to every nerve point on her body.

Everything about Bryan turned her on, and five years only made her need for him that much more desperate. Why was she thinking like this, reacting this way to him? Where was the anger? She didn't need sex, or rather she hadn't even thought about it after the last two failed fiascos. Not until now. Not until him.

Dammit, was that a grin on his face? Was he flaunting his mouthwatering assets at her on purpose? She was aroused and he knew exactly what he was doing to her. As he reached for his belt buckle, she squirmed. Next, he undid his pants and slowly slid down the zipper. While she waited to see what she suddenly ached for, she held her breath.

With a rough push, the pants slid down over his hips and his cock sprang free. It was only then she remembered he never wore underwear. What had changed was how the light sprinkling of hair on his chest had thickened and so had he, all over. His thighs were huge, his cock proportionate with his massive body, and he was thoroughly aroused. Biting her lip, she forced herself to show no emotion.

How he affected her—that much hadn't changed. Well, honestly the desire might even be more intense.

She licked her dry lips. Good Lord, had she ever taken all of him inside her? Oh, yes, sweet misery, she had. And those had been the most exquisite experiences of her life.

Hunter cleared his throat. "Uh, Bryan? Could you get on with the demo and stop showing off?"

His annoyed voice made Lacey jump. She'd been so engrossed in Bryan's naked body, she'd forgotten all about Hunter standing beside her. When he'd been naked, although she'd only seen him outlined, he'd looked just as impressive—as big and muscled as Bryan was now. She hadn't missed the absence of a tan line on all his golden skin, or that silky, shoulder length, blond hair. Both men must have had women panting after them like rock stars have groupies.

Without warning, Bryan suddenly dropped to his hands and knees, drawing her attention back to him. Light shimmered around him as the transformation turned him from man into beast. The shift happened more slowly than it had for Hunter, but within seconds, Bryan stared back at her out of golden eyes outlined in black and a broad face of furred splendor.

"Oh, my God." Surprise couldn't keep her from

admiring the pure magnificence of the cat. “Oh, Bryan, you’re s–so…beautiful.” She turned to Hunter. “He’s massive. Spectacular.”

Shocked, and in awe of his transformation, Lacey touched Hunter’s arm for support. In spite of her words of admiration and praise for Bryan, the lion let out a low jealous warning in the form of a growl.

She pulled her hand away, but relaxed when Hunter smirked. “Don’t let him intimidate you. He’d never hurt you.”

“What about you? He’s much bigger than you were. Why?”

“It’s why we’re here. It’s viral. He’s Were, a bigger version of his natural lion shifter. Before he was aware of his origins, he instinctively sought out his own kind when he approached his first change. The first time was when he turned twenty-one. While he was vulnerable, undergoing a forced shift and searching for our pack, he was attacked by a rogue shifter.

“When we found him in the first stages of his change, he was near death. Then he started having symptoms before he came back that last time. Since then we’ve had to lock him up during the full moon, and he’s getting worse with each cycle.”

“W–what do I have to do with this, this…?”

“Now he’s a danger to everyone during a full moon until he finds his mate.”

“His mate?” The idea of Bryan with another woman or lion, shifter or human, sent arrows of jealousy through her. Focusing all her attention at the large mountain lion stalking closer to her, she stared Bryan down. “What mate?” she asked, sounding a little growly herself.

Bryan let out a low sound, like a sexy purr, as Hunter's voice whispered in her ear, "You."

She gulped and straightened up. "Me?" Lacey squeaked. She anticipated that stupid nervous laugh of hers bubbling up. "How could I be his mate?"

"He told you about waking up in the desert? It was our pack he was looking for. At first he showed no signs of the Were virus, so we thought it was safe for him to be with you. We never realized he'd claimed you."

"I don't know what you mean."

"You gave him your virginity—he gave you his. You both swore undying love to one another. You're the biologist."

"Mountain lions don't mate for life."

"We're shifters. Our rules are different. His mountain lion imprinted on you years ago. You're bound to each other. There will never be another mate for him. It's as simple as that."

"Simple? I don't think so." All she kept doing was repeating his words back at them, followed by a question mark.

"I found him after the first full moon. We nursed him back to health. He checked on you all these years and for some reason you never manifested the symptoms until now. But you are infected. The CDC doesn't have any answers about your illness because they don't know about this virus."

"This isn't funny. I have a life—a ranch—a business to run if you haven't noticed."

"Had a life," Hunter corrected, but was smart enough to stay out of her reach. "Your new life will be different. We're here to help you. He couldn't let you face the fever alone."

"I'm not sure what I believe. I'm going to need more details, more evidence."

"This isn't enough?" Hunter asked and chuckled.

"Well, it's pretty overwhelming." With a glance back at Bryan, she froze.

His head leveled to hers. There was a certain familiarity in his face. No, it was the expression in his eyes. He was within reach, and her fingers ached to touch him, caress him. Did she dare reach out to him? What should she do with all her pent up feelings? Follow her heart or hold back? As if fate answered her, Bryan sat down in front of her, bent low, and nudged her hand with the top of his head like a big kitty cat. She tentatively stroked his head, loving the way he felt. The next caress was more deliberate. His soft fur and the ensuing purr seduced her.

She stood and stared into the cat's yellow eyes, speaking to the intelligence she saw there. "Bryan, this isn't simple. If you're bound to me, we're fucked." She had closed the door to her feelings for Bryan years ago. It hurt too much to go back.

The purring stopped.

"Is there someone else?" Hunter quickly asked.

Lacey flipped her attention to the man looming over her. She sniffed. He smelled remarkably like Bryan, that unusual clean pine and fresh, sundrenched air scent mixed with male. The scent both relaxed and aroused her. Maybe it was because of Bryan, or maybe it was the way all shifters smelled. She hoped not, because she was so very, very hot for it.

The threatening rumble started from deep within Bryan's enormous chest, shaking Lacey to her bones before Hunter stepped between them. Recognizing the change in the atmosphere and the danger emanating from the large cat, Lacey stepped behind Hunter.

"No. No one else," Lacey hurriedly answered, but it was too late. She saw the lion's eyes narrow, going from Bryan's conscious human mind to pure animal instinct. The cat took control from Bryan and snarled, his muscles bunching to attack. As everything human dissolved into the lion, Bryan slapped at Hunter to reach his mate.

Hunter backed up and pushed her to safety further behind him. She tumbled off to the side and let out a squeal. Hunter shifted in the time it took Lacey to blink.

Half expecting the cats to turn on her once she'd fallen, she scrambled up on a boulder.

The lions leapt into the air, their powerful bodies slamming into each other. The sound of their deafening roars filled the air, echoing inside the cave as they rolled in each other's grasp and ripped at each other with their large teeth and sharp claws.

The men were gone. There was no humanity left within them. The beasts were in charge now.

Throughout the mêlée, Lacey thought she saw the men occasionally trying to morph back into their human forms. If one of them succeeded before the other, it could mean certain death.

Bryan, larger by far, eventually took advantage of his size. He had the edge over Hunter, who was weakening from several serious lacerations. Bryan took the opportunity and jumped.

Hunter dropped to the cave floor, trying to shift.

"No, Bryan!" she screamed. Before she could think, Lacey reacted. Stepping forward, she faced down

Bryan and protected Hunter from his brother's attack. Then drawing Bryan away from the wounded man, she walked away from Hunter forcing Bryan's eyes to follow her.

He had time to settle down before she inched her way to back to Hunter's side. When he stared up at her and made eye contact, something inside her trembled. A warm flush ran through her body and her mind opened to his. She thought she heard him say, "mine" as he lifted his hand and touched her face.

In that instant, something between them connected, and Hunter—part man, part beast—purred.

Bryan roared. The lion's attention shifted between her and Hunter. Then he turned to her, sniffed and hissed when he met her eye to eye.

Bryan growled and stalked her as she backed up.

Hunter's warning was weak. "Don't move. And for God's sake, don't run."

As if she could, trapped as she was, with the big lion gaining on her and the rock wall behind her. Instead, she tried to back up slowly.

Her knowledge about animal behavior taught her enough to know better. But being faced with a mountain lion of humongous size made it hard to ignore instinct. The urge to run was ingrained in prey.

The lion focused on her as Hunter finished shifting. He was bleeding heavily, but to her relief, his wounds began healing almost at once.

"Bryan," she whispered. She had to believe he wouldn't hurt her. Right. Just when she recalled how he'd emotionally hurt her before, the big cat knocked her on her ass and stood over her, sniffing her like she was his next meal.

"Bryan, shift. Dammit, shift, now." Hunter shouted the order before he collapsed. Something in his command must have reached Bryan because he backed off.

Albeit, she had to admit he moved all too reluctantly. With his cat belly dragging on the cave floor, he crawled in reverse on all fours. Obviously annoyed at the demand and partly in frustration, he opened his mouth and roared, but remained in control, at least enough not to do any serious damage.

As he moved away, closer to his clothes and the light, Lacey risked inhaling.

Finally, he shimmered back into the man, the one she recognized and had once loved, the one who could take her breath away with a thought. He was also the one man she swore she wouldn't risk her heart or her life for again. Too bad he was already wheedling his way back into both. *Dammit.* She forced herself to think about what she'd lost and the years she'd suffered.

As their gazes met this time, she saw regret and the sorrow in his eyes. His voice cracked, thick with emotion when he asked, "Are you all right?"

"Fine." She brushed herself off, checking herself out. "I'm bruised, but not seriously injured. Check on Hunter. He hasn't moved."

She looked over at Bryan's friend who was still sprawled on the floor, naked and human again. They both rushed to him.

"Hunter?" she called. His injuries looked as if they were healed, but he hadn't gotten up after he collapsed.

Bryan picked up Hunter by the shoulders and cradled him. "What have I done?"

"I–is he…dead?" Lacey asked, placing a hand to

his pulse. The dread reached deeper than she expected, a sharp pain stabbing deep inside her. Then the man moaned. “Thank God,” she exclaimed. A shiver of relief ran through her. And another sensation she couldn’t explain. Desire.

****

Hunter opened his eyes and sighed. “Tell me you aren’t going to kiss me, Bryan.”

“Bryan won’t, but I may!” Lacey patted his cheek and smiled.

Bryan’s chest rumbled again with that low, jealous sound.

“Uh, just an expression, Bryan. Chill,” she said. “Thank you for trying to protect me, Hunter.”

“Yeah, for now.” Hunter sat up, rubbed his head, and gave her a strange look. He managed a sarcastic smile for Bryan, but his voice sounded weak. “We have a problem.”

“I know. I’m sorry.” Bryan grunted and dropped his face in his hands. “I don’t know what else to say.” He stood up, helping Hunter off the floor, and touched a large scratch on Hunter’s arm. “The virus. I’ve infected you.”

“Yeah, maybe. There’s that,” he said. “We’ll see if I start manifesting the symptoms next full moon.” Hunter tried to take a few steps in Lacey’s direction, but seemed to think about what he was doing and stopped. “But that’s not all.”

Lacey looked at him differently. Her eyes sparkled with… If Hunter didn’t know better, he’d swear it was lust. The cat inside him purred with satisfaction while the man ached with regret for his brother. Bryan had already suffered so much, now he’d have to face sharing his mate—at least through her transition. "I think my cat imprinted on Lacey. She may have responded."

Bryan glowered at Hunter and then scrutinized Lacy's expression. Hunter watched his brother's face and recognized the moment he realized Lacey had reacted to his bond. Her scent was already different and heat radiated off her like a brand. Bryan's eyes narrowed.

"Not sure what you two are insinuating." She shook herself out of her reverie and Hunter saw the scientist in Lacey kick in. She looked at her watch. "Well, as interesting as all this has been, I have a few arrangements to make before tomorrow. I've got to get going."

"That's it?" Hunter chuckled, thinking 'great self-control'. "You learn all this and remain calm and collected." He shook his head in disbelief.

"I'd like time to assimilate what I've seen and experienced. I'd like to take notes, but I really do have quite a bit to do before the reunion. So if you both wouldn't mind getting dressed…?"

"We'll ride back with you," Bryan said, ignoring Hunter and pulling on his pants. "Do you mind putting us up at the ranch?"

Hunter quickly added, "We'll pay and help with chores. I can't stand Bryan's snoring, and now with the full moon issue approaching, you'll need us."

"I guess… If what you claim is true, I don't want to face the fever alone." Lacey paused as if considering what more she could add to her statement, then with a noncommittal expression said, "After all, you are here to help me."

"Right. It'll be easier if we're with you," Hunter said with a wink to put her at ease. "It'll work out better for all of us. The horses will need a place to run and so will we."

Bryan stood and cleared his voice. He put both hands on Lacey's shoulders, forcing her to look at him. "Thank you, Lacey. I'm so sorry for… Hell, for screwing up your life and… And I swear I'll make it up to you."

Hunter could tell by the hitch in Bryan's voice and the soulful expression in his eyes he meant every word of his apology…and Hunter agreed. He was sorry too for what they were going to face.

"I know," she said. "I don't blame you for infecting me. You didn't even know what you were, let alone understand the consequences of our actions."

And based on Bryan's reaction, Hunter was certain she had to know he never would have risked her life.

"I'm also sure when they discover who is to blame for my father's death, the blame won't be placed at your feet."

A commitment for more seemed premature, despite how her insides ached for Bryan's touch. "You find out who killed my father, and we'll call it even."

"Deal."

"Things were about to change drastically anyway without this complication." Hunter seemed determined to explain.

"What?" Lacey turned to Bryan then to Hunter. "What does that mean?"

Bryan stood in front of her. "I came back to tell you as soon as I found out about your fevers. I was going to tell you after Hunter demonstrated and…well, before I lost control."

"You want the bad news now or later?" Hunter asked tentatively.

"There's more?" Lacey asked. "Worse?"

"Well, it depends on whose viewpoint you're in." Hunter broadened his grin.

"No. Don't tell me. I don't think I could stand anything else."

"Don't worry. What Bryan's stuttering around is that we came here to help you through your transition."

"Wha–at transition?" Their words worried her, but she refused to panic.

"You've been feeling different lately. Hotter. Skin crawling, fevers, blackouts, aching all over?"

No, she wasn't giving in, not accepting everything they said without thinking the situation through. But deep in her heart, she understood that not admitting the symptoms Hunter described—the ones that were exactly what she'd been experiencing—wasn't going to make them go away.

Bryan touched her cheek. The gesture was both familiar and devastating.

"It's going to happen, whether you want it to or not. We can help you through this. God, Lacey, I don't want you to go through this first time alone."

"What's going to happen? I thought I was infected with the fever, like you?" Adrenaline pumped through her. *Like him?* Her heart rate picked up and so did her fear. What they weren't telling her scared her more than what they were saying. "Maybe someone should explain what this all means, and then we can work on a plan to fix it."

"There's no fixing it, Lacey. If I'd known what I

was doing to you that last time…" He shook his head. "I won't lie to you. I don't know if I'd have done anything differently. But I'm sorry for what this means to your life. You've already lost so much."

"The past is behind us," she said.

"Yeah, we have to focus on the future," Hunter said.

"Charming as this little reunion has been, Bryan, I'm not ready to give up my research and my ranch to play house kitty to two mountain lions."

Bryan looked grim while Hunter maintained his good humor. "You won't mind if we try to change your mind, will you?"

Lacey ignored the question and gave the two luscious hunks a once-over. There was something to be said for both men if you ignored their bossy attitude.

"Lacey, like it or not, you are going to shift with the next full moon."

She waved off Hunter's words, not wanting to hear any more. "I'm afraid of what's ahead, what you're not telling me. So spit it out, dammit." As much as she hated to admit it, he was right. Too many unexplained changes in her body and her senses had manifested over recent months. Too many to ignore.

"The change has already started. We can smell your scent."

She scrunched up her nose. "Yuck."

"It's definitely not 'yuck' to us." He tilted his head at Bryan. "He can barely contain himself around you, and now that my lion imprinted on you, neither can I."

"Fine, fine, hang around, but no change."

"Sorry, darlin' there's no force on Earth that will prevent it."

"I mean, I have a life and, such as it is, it's mine. I may shift, but my life can't change. I'll have to make shifting fit in." She pulled the band from her shoulder length hair, shook it free, and combed her fingers through it.

"I'm not sure how we'll fit in," Hunter said with a worried scowl on his face.

"We'll see." Bryan didn't look any happier.

"If this is going to be a relationship, and not just a seasonal mating between the three of us, we better spend time learning about each other." She knew nothing about Hunter and had five years of misgivings to get over with Bryan.

Hunter took her hand in his. "Good idea. I think we should date."

"Date?" Lacey and Bryan repeated.

"Together?" Lacey asked, looking at both men.

"As in a threesome?" Bryan asked incredulously.

"Two. Three. However. Whenever, bro."

Hunter was cute when he was serious.

"He's right. I need to find out about Hunter and you. Like, how much has all this changed you, Bryan?"

"I'm a fucking part-time mountain lion. How do you think it's affected me? I'm more aggressive."

"Really?" Lacey stared at him blankly. "As if you even had to mention that little bit of insight…"

He shrugged the tension from his shoulders. "But I'm working on my control. I'm getting better. I think. Usually, I'm better than this," he added when she rolled her eyes.

"What about you, Hunter. Have you always been with the pride?"

"Yes. When we were babies, our parents were on a

hunt. I'd wandered off on my own before some ranch hands stumbled across Bryan, who was obediently playing with his truck where Mom and Dad left us."

"So you really are biological brothers?" They did look enough alike for her to believe it. Apparently, Bryan hadn't meant "brother" as a euphemism after all.

"Yes," Hunter said. "Our pride looked for Bryan for years without a trace. When he wandered back into our territory, we found him too late to help him through his first transition and too late to prevent the Were infection. Once he found out how the shifter gene can be passed during unprotected sex, he tried to find answers and a way to prevent it from happening to you."

Bryan touched her cheek. "I checked back on you every year. Had Thomas promise to call if anything happened to you."

"When I get my hands on that man…"

"Don't blame him. I told him it was for your own good. I hoped maybe you'd somehow escaped. Then this year you started manifesting early symptoms."

"How did you know?" she asked Bryan.

"Thomas called and Hunter's been in touch with Doc."

"Doc wouldn't say anyth—"

"Not intentionally, and not directly about you, but Hunter claimed he was from the CDC. He asked Doc if he had a case that fit the symptoms and requested a blood sample. Wasn't hard to guess it was you."

Lacey's scowl incorporated both men. "Like I said, I have things to do. I hope you brought formal clothes. The country club is hosting the diamond jubilee party, and I don't want my dates to be underdressed."

# Chapter Ten

The day had been eventful, what with so many tourists and reunion visitors in town. The gala tonight, after the parades and dinner, was what they'd all been waiting for; a chance to get everyone together in one location and watch how they interacted.

Bryan was used to hanging with the country club set from his past, but Hunter had to learn if he wanted to work in high end real estate, he'd have to mingle with high end clients. As an attorney, Bryan had the contacts, but whether he liked the idea or not, he and Hunter worked their business together. The country clubs and elite parties Hunter had attended in the past were no more or less exclusive than this one. Both men fit right in with the Cauldwell Country Club set.

Hunter hung back with a drink in his hand and admired the way Lacey mingled and managed a smile for everyone, including the three women with Tory Cauldwell. The brunette seemed especially put out by her. She must be the one who had her mind set on snagging Bryan. She gave Lacey a limp wrist when they greeted. As an afterthought, she added an air kiss on both cheeks, but Hunter suspected it was only because Bryan was standing beside her.

Hunter couldn't resist asking Lacey to dance, and he enjoyed watching the women's heads spin on their necks like they were on a swivel. Their attention shot between Tory, Bryan, and himself, drawing instant conclusions. There was no question he and Bryan looked too much alike for anyone to ignore the similarities. Rumors would run rampant, and Hunter couldn't wait for the reaction from Tory's old man.

Lacey politely excused herself and took his hand. "I'd love to dance, thank you," she said. She didn't introduce him and neither did Bryan. Ignoring the group's unexpressed questions regarding his identity, Lacey smiled graciously as they turned away.

He pulled her against him and whispered in her ear, "Well, that went over like a fart in church. Everyone smelled it but everyone's ignoring it."

She giggled against his chest when he pulled her into his arms and two stepped to the music. "Jeanette is grinding her teeth with curiosity and Carol Anne is spittin' jealous. Thanks for saving me."

"From what?"

"Carol Anne always wanted a Cauldwell and had to settle for Tory. Jeanette wanted Bryan. Now she can't believe there are two of you. You know, two men as hunky as Bryan, and I showed up with both of you."

"Who's the other woman with them?"

"That's my friend, Donna," she said.

"What's a friend of yours doing hanging out with them?" Hunter kept his disapproval to himself. It didn't seem to bother Lacey that her friend was associating with the *so-called* enemy.

"Donna was born into the country club set, but that never kept her from being a friend. She was a couple of grades ahead of me in school and always marched to a different beat than the rest of those snooty girls." Lacey leaned in and whispered, "We hit it off and grew closer over the last few years. Now she's mingling, doing some reconnaissance for me."

Hunter glanced over to where Carol Anne had abandoned Tory and slipped her arm into Bryan's. She and Jeanette were circling Bryan like vultures that hadn't seen roadkill in a month.

Lacey put her head down and let out a low, unladylike sound, tensing all over.

"You have to put up with them much?" Hunter asked.

"All my life," she said. "You get used to it and then you get over it."

"With all you've been through, you have a great attitude, Lacey."

"Not always, where they're concerned. I see it this way: they're still wannabes, and I have my horse riding business, my teaching position, and good friends. When I look at their lives…well, it's sad. But if they don't take their hands off Bryan, their lives are going to get even sadder."

Just before Hunter thought there was going to be a cat fight—literally—Donna, Lacey's Barbie doll spy, went to Bryan's rescue. The other women were left standing around with Tory whispering under their breath. As soon as Donna dragged Bryan onto the dance floor, Hunter and Lacey both released a sigh, and then Lacey relaxed in his arms.

"Hunter, let's get a drink. I know the bartender."

"Who is this bartender and how well do you know him?" Was that jealousy Hunter was feeling? He'd have to examine this sudden sense of ownership he felt toward Lacey.

"Jack, Keiran's husband. He works for the sheriff's

department." Lacey furrowed her brow and gave Hunter a sideways glance as if he'd lost his mind.

Hunter shrugged. Yes, he was losing his mind. He'd never cared about any woman's past.

"Duh, I've known him almost all my life like everyone else in this town. Keiran's husband works for the caterer sometimes when he can arrange it."

"Oh, right." Hunter grunted, feeling stupid and confused. "So Jack is bartending?"

"Play your cards right and I'll get you a beer. I want to introduce you to him anyway and check in with him. He's supposed to be keeping his ears open for me. With all the people back in town for the celebration, I figured a few well-placed questions might offer some new information about what happened back…"

"So let me get this straight. You have Donna, the goddess, spying for you. Jack, Keiran's detective husband, Bryan, and I all gathering information for you. Anyone else we should know about?" Hunter asked.

"Well, yes. Thomas, of course."

"Right, Thomas. Does Bryan know any of this?"

She shrugged. "I didn't think to mention it. I suppose he should know we have help."

"Good idea. Will probably keep us from stepping on each other's toes. Now how about that beer?"

As they wandered arm in arm to the bar, Hunter observed Donna and Bryan stop and talk to a man in uniform. Bryan told Hunter he'd dropped by the sheriff's office several weeks before to explain his disappearance. A falling out with old man Cauldwell and discovering he was adopted explained a lot.

When Lacey sighed, Hunter turned to see what was bothering her. She watched Jack as he fixed a few drinks. Nothing appeared strange. "What?"

"Jack will probably be doing a lot more moonlighting once Keiran gets pregnant. Then she won't be able to keep up with the riding lessons later on."

"You worried about help? What will you do without her?"

"No, the help isn't the issue. Keiran's got a mess of younger sisters. Two or three of them already help out in season. We're just winding down from the summer influx of tourists. The dude ranches were packed this year. They always need horses and extra guides."

"Then what's bothering you?"

"I wish I could find something for Keiran to do when she can't ride. They'll need the extra income."

"Don't worry," Hunter said, as they approached the bar. "If I have learned anything about you tonight, it's that you'll think of something. Now, is this Jack?"

"Jack Tatum, Hunter Harris," Lacey said, making the introductions. Jack stared at Hunter then glanced in Bryan's direction.

"Pleased to meet you. Harris? Don't recall any Harris kin to the Cauldwells."

"He's Bryan's biological brother. It's a long story."

Jack lowered his voice. "Then I guess that's what has Tory and his father in a fit tonight. Something about most of the land the ranch sits on belonging to Cauldwell's first wife. Seems the codicil in her will left her land to Bryan, not her husband. Tory's fuming."

"But Bryan wasn't her natural son. Why would she do that?"

"She loved him like he was her own." Jack stood back. "Hold that thought while I take care of these payin' customers." He moved down the bar to serve an older couple. The man left a ten in the tip jar and waved to Lacey. Jack told him he'd name his firstborn after him. "My dad," he explained.

The younger man's humor made Hunter laugh. He could see why Lacey trusted him.

"Where was I? Oh, yeah. From all I remember, Missus Cauldwell was a good, loving woman. Even the old man wasn't so bad back when she was alive. After he took up with Tory's mom, things went to hell. Now that woman he married was known as the wicked witch of west Texas."

"So now that Bryan's back…are you telling us the ranch is his?" Hunter wanted clarification. Bryan had no idea.

"Seems so. At least the land that Emma bequeathed to him." Jack released a slow smile. "Guess the Cauldwells will lose the parcel out by you, Lacey. Looks like they lost the land with the hills and the oil. Couldn't happen to a nicer group of scoundrels."

Hunter wondered, "Who else knows about the old will?"

"I have no idea. It had to be recorded, so there's a record somewhere. It's not common knowledge, I can tell you that much. Tory and the old man were whispering and shut up fast when I moved in their direction."

"You heard them from here?" Lacey asked. "Maybe you misunderstood."

"No. I heard them just right. I have exceptional hearing." Jack squirmed and changed the subject. "Hope this helps. Tomorrow I'm going to look into all this, Lacey. Seems secrets like this open all kinds of cans of worms, if you get my drift. Nice meeting you, Hunter."

"Yeah, you, too, and thanks for the heads up." Hunter discreetly sniffed the air and swore he caught the faint scent of dog. No, wolf. The bowls of potpourri strewn about the long bar affected Hunter's sense of smell. Nice cover. He and Bryan weren't the only dual life-forms present.

"You know, I don't know how Keiran stands Jack's new aftershave. It makes me think of sandalwood and wet dog," Lacey said.

Hunter began to chuckle.

"What's so funny?"

He wasn't sure he should share this new information with Lacey yet. Apparently, her sense of smell was developing, but he didn't think she was ready to hear her girlfriend was married to a wolf shifter. Once he opened his senses, he realized the place was crawling with other life forms. The tables were spread with fragrant fruits, like pineapples, and strong-scented flowers, like gardenias, to interfere with their highly developed olfactory organs. Who or what were hiding their identities?

Lacey stiffened beside him. He followed her gaze to a man arguing with Bryan. Donna glanced back at them and he assumed she needed help. Lacey didn't move when Hunter asked, "Is that Cauldwell?"

Lacey nodded and inhaled. She straightened her back and said, "Come. Bryan needs support."

Hunter wondered if he did. Things had changed since Bryan left, but Lacey didn't know that. She was used to supporting him after his adoptive father beat him down; ever since Bryan defied his father and continued to date her in spite of the family's objections.

Hunter understood what Bryan saw in her over other women. As he appraised the women in the garden, he realized their looks were merely a forgery of Lacey's true beauty. He didn't want to add to her problems. She had enough to deal with standing up to the Cauldwells, and Bryan had enough on his mind with Lacey. Wait until he found out about the family ranch situation and the influx of the other shifters into town.

Some could be susceptible to the Were virus. And if they'd been here all along, Hunter couldn't help wondering if one of them had been responsible for Lacey's father's death. He figured the news could wait a little longer.

"Okay, Lacey, let's go save our boy from the big bad wolf. Though, truth be told, we're probably saving the Cauldwells from Bryan."

This would give him the opportunity to find out what Cauldwell was, if he could get close enough.

Tory walked up to Cauldwell around the same time Hunter pulled aside his brother. Good, Hunter thought, he nailed a two for one special.

"Hey, Bryan. Can I have a word with you?" Hunter asked, maneuvering himself closer to the old man and Tory. But even after he opened up his enhanced olfactory senses, there was no scent of dog.

"Yeah, you go have a talk with him," Tory said with that ferret-looking sneer on his face. "Tell him he should have stayed gone after he disappeared."

Bryan released that low growl Hunter knew signified a loss of control. If Bryan let it slip, they'd all be in deep shit. "Bro, not here." We have something you need to hear."

Things were piling up. It was getting late and, sooner or later, Hunter was going to have to come clean about the other shifters. For now, he and Lacey should give Bryan the good news about the ranch.

Lacey, bless her heart, jumped right between Bryan and his father. "Sorry to interrupt your little homecoming, sir—and you, too, Tory—apparently Bryan has a business call." The lie spilled naturally past her lips before she turned away and walked off arm in arm with Bryan.

Hunter followed, repressing a chuckle when she asked, "What is it you two do for a living anyway? I don't recall you mentioning."

"Why don't you make something up? It couldn't sound any more truthful than the lies pouring out of your mouth," Bryan said. "You're too good at this."

"She may have to get better. Wait until you hear what we found out, Bryan," Hunter said.

"To answer your question, Lacey, I'm a real estate developer. Bryan did go back to school, got his law degree, and passed the bar. He's one of the best real estate attorneys in the state."

"Sounds like an oxymoron—best and attorney don't belong in the same sentence," she said with a grin.

"Really? Lawyer jokes?" Bryan asked.

"Actually, I can't think of a better profession for you, not with what you two are about to face," she said to them.

"Yup, we're just the boys to handle it." Hunter sneered. He may have sounded cocky, but there was damn good reason for that. The Harrises were very successful. The Cauldwells wouldn't know what hit them when they were finished with them.

"Where do you want to go to talk?" Bryan asked. "Out back?"

"No, not anywhere around here," Hunter spit out then switched to their mental link. *"This town is crawling with...shifters and more. Don't you smell them?"*

*"No."* Bryan sniffed and his eyes narrowed in Lacey's direction. *"My senses are overwhelmed with Lacey's scent. I can't focus on anything else. Who?"*

*"I don't know these people,"* Hunter thought, but looked in the direction of the bar. "I met Keiran's husband. He's an interesting sort. '*Wolf.*' "

"Jack?" Bryan stared over at the bar. *"Must have gone through his change after I left."*

"Nice guy. Full of useful information." Hunter nodded. "Have you tried the pineapple?"

"I'm not much for pineapple." *"Doesn't pineapple interfere with our sense of smell?"*

"That's good." Hunter nodded again. *"Stay away from the gardenias and the potpourri on the bar, too."* "I don't think they agree with you."

"What are you two talking about?" Lacey broke in, confusion written in her expression. "Why do I feel there's more going on between you than you're letting on?"

"There is," Hunter whispered. "We need to find some place to talk, privately. Not here," he clarified, glancing in the Cauldwells' direction.

"Come this way," Hunter said. "Let's go see Thomas." Dragging Lacey along to where Thomas stood by the gate, he figured meeting him was a good enough reason to wander to the far end of the veranda.

"I'm not sure I'm speaking to that—" Lacey folded her arms across her chest.

"How about we get out of here, Lacey? I think I put in enough time," Bryan said. "Say goodnight to Thomas. You can't stay mad at your best friend for looking out for you all these years."

"There's still plenty to do before I can go home."

"I'll help, if you forgive me," Thomas said. "No one will expect you to stay."

"I've been trying to get her out of here for the last half hour." Bryan frowned at him. "I figured we'd make a clean break when Tory and Cauldwell cornered me."

"How'd you escape? They heard you were back and from what Jack said, the shit hit the fan."

"The old man knew where I was for two years and didn't have much to say. Then, later, you were the only one who knew where to find me, Thomas."

"Lacey are you going to speak to me?" Thomas asked. "I've never kept anything else from you, hon. Bryan said he loved you and it was for your own good. I thought if he loved you that much I should trust him. Forgive me?"

Lacey unfolded her arms and walked into Thomas's open arms. "Forgiven! But don't you ever hide anything from me again."

For an instant, Thomas's expression went flat. Hunter had to admit the guy rebounded well. "Does that mean you want to hear all about the dream I had about you and me last night?"

Lacey closed her eyes and covered her ears. "Nah, nah. Nah, nah. Is he gone yet?"

"All right," Thomas uncovered her ears. "I'm just chiding."

A few steps away from the exit, a light wind blew across the terrace carrying Lacey's scent on the breeze. A rumble he had to fight down rose in Hunter's throat. What with the Were virus infecting him and the full moon approaching, his inner cat was growing more aggressive by the minute. If only there was a way to ease them into accepting the idea of a ménage bond before Lacey's transition made it a necessity.

Hunter pulled Bryan aside. "Meet me back at the cave, after you finish making excuses to the cleanup committee."

"What is it?" Bryan asked Hunter. "You seem out of control."

"Testy is all. You'll understand when I tell you what Jack said."

The shape of Lacey's pupils had already started to change. The tilt to her naturally almond shaped eyes made her look all the more exotic. The changes were subtle but he didn't miss the way she walked with more catlike grace.

*"Later, bro. Look at her and the way the men are eyeballing her. For God's sake, get her out of here."*

"What?" Lacey asked.

"Nothing we can talk about here." Hunter brushed her question off and pleaded with Thomas. "Convince her it's okay to leave."

*"She is going to grow more and more unstable before dawn."* Hunter used their mental link so only Bryan would hear his warning. "*We have to get her out of here. We're running out of time."*

Her feminine stride already turned into the confident glide of the cat. Silent. Smooth. Slinky. Sexy as hell.

Hunter noticed the nuances of the lioness rising to the surface. The other men noticed, too. They couldn't tear their attention away from her even though they didn't understand what was drawing them to her.

*"I'm having a hard time keeping the lion from surfacing and tearing apart every guy in the place who's staring at her."*

*"The men can't help themselves. Look at her eyes, the way she walks."*

Bryan grumbled under his breath, "I don't know why we have to hang around, Lacey."

"I hate leaving the rest to clean up—" she said.

*"Bryan, there's more you should know, and we have a lot to explain to her tonight."*

Thomas placed both hands on her shoulder and turned her toward Bryan. "You've done more than your fair share. Now scoot."

*"Tell Thomas she has a fever. He'll make her excuses."*

"She still has that fever," Bryan said and stared at Thomas, giving him a friendly pat on the back.

"Still? If you have a fever, you should rest." Thomas said, shooing her away. "Go on. We'll handle the cleanup. Don't worry. Donna loves ordering me around."

Hunter jumped in before Lacey voiced another objection. "Okay, then, let's get going."

"What now?"

"I'll tell you later." Hunter resorted to their mental link for privacy. "*I'd rather discuss this in private. The lioness is rising. She's getting closer. When you come, make sure you bring Lacey. This concerns her.*"

*"I'll meet you there in less than an hour. I can't*

*stand this much longer."*

If Lacey thought she was angry about Bryan binding her to him without her knowledge, she was going to be furious when she found out about what their connection would mean. Hunter wished they had more time—time to get to know each other. Time was up. There was no way he'd make it through the full moon without her and she wouldn't survive her transition without both of them now.

## Chapter Eleven

"You feeling any better, Lacey?" Hunter asked. "By the way, you look great tonight."

"Thank you. I'm feeling okay. You know about the side effect of the fevers?"

He nodded.

"Well, I'm also hot. Itchy. Honestly, I'm glad to be away from town and out here where it's cooler. I feel better."

Bryan stepped forward. "Hunter, Lacey told me what Jack said about Emma Cauldwell's will. What's with all the secrecy?"

"It's not about the will."

"The others?"

"No, Bryan." Hunter backed away from them, deciding it would be better to start by spitting out the news. "I confirmed I have the Were virus."

"Shit! I'm sorry," Bryan said, shaking his head, "Real sorry. I hoped you'd be able to fight it off. But you should be fine until you find a mate—"

"No. Hold off. There's more."

"More?"

"Yeah." Hunter paused before he ran his hand down his face. "And it's real bad." Hunter backed up, glancing between Lacey and Bryan. "Lacey, would you mind standing in front of Bryan?"

"Enough. Just spit it out," Bryan snarled.

"Okay. When Lacey saved my life," Hunter looked ready to bolt, "not only did my lion imprint on her, her cat responded."

"What!" Bryan lunged, and Lacey gasped at the same time. She held her arms out, again protecting Hunter from Bryan as the anger vibrated around them. Hunter watched the lion morph beneath the surface of Bryan's skin as he fought to keep his lion under control.

"Sorry to complicate everything. Hey, you remember how we dated the same woman or two in the past, right? It can't be that different than—"

"Ew!" Lacey said.

Hunter realized his mistake immediately. Maybe mentioning how the little fox shifter wanted both of them wasn't such a good idea. Hunter thought it would help them ease into the discussion of a possible ménage relationship, but Lacey seemed repulsed and Bryan looked embarrassed.

Clearly, the picture of the two men pleasuring another woman disgusted Lacey. Her respiration increased. The idea of Bryan with another woman made her inner cat furious. Besides almost breaking her heart with that little tidbit about them both dating the same woman, he was right, her lioness wanted them both. Hunter sensed her jealousy in so many ways. The heat boiled up inside her and rolled off in waves around her. He swore he heard her spit.

"Thanks, Hunter! How is talking about shit like that gonna help me out here?" Bryan asked, looking like he'd like to punch him.

Instead, he turned to Lacey and tried to explain. "Sorry. Hunter's got it all wrong. Sometimes we dated the same women. I tried to… Hell, I didn't…

Couldn't…" He stepped closer and cupped her chin.

Hunter noted his brother's touch took her off guard.

Bryan looked deep into her eyes and said, "I haven't been with anyone else."

Hunter couldn't believe what he was hearing. "Ever?" he asked, astounded.

"Never," Bryan whispered, still staring at Lacey.

"It's none of my business what you've done these last five years." She twisted out of his grasp. Her voice sounded brittle, almost as brittle as Hunter felt.

This was going to be a mess.

Bryan held her in place and forced her to hear him out. "Yes, it is, Lacey. I pledged my love to you and that hasn't changed. My emotional and my physical love. My heart, as well as my body, remain yours."

"You never…?" Hunter asked Bryan, incredulous.

"No," Bryan snapped and shook his head. "I have no desire for anyone. Just her."

"Shit!"

As unbelievable as it was, the impact of what Bryan admitted made Hunter shudder. "Suddenly I see what I'm in for. Insane changes during the full moon. And no sex."

"No sex?"

"No sex." Hunter took a chance and turned to Bryan. "I'm not ready."

On their mental path, he tried to explain, "*Not until you and I are sure we can share your mate. One, you're my brother and I won't fight you. Two, somehow I have to convince Lacey this is right. I don't want to be a third wheel once a month at the full moon. I want a mate who wants me because she loves me, not because she feels sorry for me. Though how I'm supposed to manage courting her, convincing you, and adjusting to being an imprinted male, while I stay in enough control to help you with Lacey's change, I don't know. God give me the strength."*

Bryan promised to be the one to tell her what was going to happen to her. Now Hunter had a more personal stake in the matter. He wanted Lacey to care about him and being the bearer of more bad tidings wouldn't immediately ingratiate him to her. Bottom line was he didn't want a mate who loved his brother and only fucked him once a month to keep him sane.

Hunter ran a hand through his hair and paced, thinking long and hard about the horrible torture Bryan had endured to stay away from his mate to protect her. "Geez Bryan, it's no wonder you've been in a bad mood for five years."

"Well, that makes two of us," Lacey admitted. "At least now there's a reasonable explanation for my own failed attempts at sex."

Bryan's growl rumbled and Hunter quickly interrupted. "She said attempts. Failed attempts, bro."

He risked looking away from Bryan to glance at her. "I had no say in this. I wouldn't hurt you, either of you. You must know that."

"Exactly what does all this mean?" Lacey asked, waving her hands in a circle incorporating the three of them.

"I'm yours." Hunter shrugged his broad shoulders and tried to look meek. "I have to be honest. I'm not sorry it's you my cat imprinted on."

Lacey had to admit the look, when he spoke directly to her, had its merits. Charisma. He had it in spades. She had questions, too many to voice, but the first she managed through tight lips. “How could your lion imprint on me without us having sexual contact or either of us saying the binding words? You told me that’s what bound Bryan and I.”

Hunter stared at Lacey, giving her his sexiest smile. “I guess when you offered your life up for me, my lion took that as sign enough. We may not be bound the way you and Bryan are, but my cat has a mind of his own.”

“Well, so do I.” She fisted her hands on her hips to keep from punching something…or someone.

“Seems now you’re destined to be both our mates.”

That did it. Her fingers twitched and her hands balled up. “Well, think again.” She shook her head at Hunter to make her point and did her best to stay calm.

“I can see you haven’t gotten used to the idea yet. I’ll wait until the idea settles. Until we’re all comfortable with the situation,” Hunter said, backing up with a teasing sparkle in his eyes.

“Don’t hold your breath,” Lacey said through clenched teeth. No one, neither of them, could go around claiming her. She was a grown woman with responsibilities.

Hunter looked entirely too pleased from Lacey’s point of view, and the low grumble at her side meant Bryan wholeheartedly agreed with her.

“Wipe that shit-eatin’ grin off your face. You don’t have to look so damned pleased about it,” Bryan snapped.

“I swear I’ll go through the full moon cycle chained forever if necessary,” Hunter said. “Unless…she wants me.”

The rumbling in Bryan's throat increased. His internal lion started a low, threatening growl. Annoyed with the whole incident and the possessive jealousy thing, too, Lacey backhanded Bryan's shoulder.

"Not again." She released an exasperated sigh. "Shut up, Bryan. Hasn't your jealous cat caused enough problems?"

For a moment, his growl went deeper, like a complaint, but the growl turned into silence when she stood up and started pacing. At least he was smart enough to know when to back off. Instead of fear, she felt pissed. The men acted as if she didn't have any say in the matter.

"Either we're all in this together, or we're all fucked," Hunter said.

"Unless one of us dies," Bryan mentioned in a flat tone.

"That's not exactly my first choice for a solution. What about you, Bryan?" Lacey asked. "You ready to see Hunter dead?"

"No, don't worry. We won't fight to the death." Bryan managed to say that without a growl and with a straight face.

"He's right." Hunter chuckled as if it was funny or something. "You'll both just have to put up with me taking on the monthly imprisonment and a lifetime of *surly.* Let me tell you, payback might be fun after putting up with Bryan's cranky attitude for five years."

Bryan's jealousy ruled his head, and anger ruled hers. Hunter was the only one trying to be lighthearted about the dilemma even if he wasn't being entirely sensible about goading Bryan.

"Okay, no deaths, no imprisonments, and no

lifetime of bad moods. How do we solve this problem?" Lacey asked. When did she become the voice of reason in this paranormal fantasy?

"Do you want me?" Hunter asked.

Lacey flushed, a dead giveaway to her feelings. "What kind of question is that?" Why did the thought appeal to her? Dammit. Why hadn't she learned how to play poker?

"Okay, then we'll have to figure out a way to share you."

Share her? She had to stop them from thinking of her as theirs. She didn't belong to them. She wasn't a horse or a car. "There you go, again, talking like there are no other options—like I don't have any say in the matter."

"You don't," they said in unison.

"We'll see about that. Bryan, you and Hunter can stand there all day, naked as the day you were born, but I'm going to go soak my aching muscles in the mineral springs. If you want to talk, let me know when you're ready. That's where you'll find me."

****

Rewinding and securing her hair off her neck, she didn't look back as she made her way through the tunnel. She took the one to the grotto, where the hot, mineral pool bubbled in invitation.

"Since she belongs with both of us now, it will be even better—" Hunter sounded like he was already making plans.

"Fuck that! What happened to you backing off and giving her time?"

"Smell her scent? She wants me. I think she'll need me."

"I haven't even settled things between the two of us and you're already honing in—"

"Hold on right there," Hunter said. "I'm not honing in. This isn't what I had in mind for your homecoming."

"Me either." Bryan scrubbed a hand down his face.

"Did she say 'talk'?"

"Yeah, just talk, Hunter."

"Not likely if she takes off that top," Hunter whispered softly. The low rumble of desire was hard to miss.

Bryan's eyes narrowed, and he licked his lips. "Hunter, I just love talking to a woman who takes charge."

"Since when? Bryan, you're alpha through and through."

"Since her." He glanced in the direction Lacey took and groaned.

"Yeah, but are you going to be all right with me and her?"

"Under normal circumstances? No. But Hunter, she's my mate. My alpha female. Our bond forces me to see to her needs, no matter what I feel. Maybe her lioness did imprint on you and …"

"If so, she'll need me as much as she needs you. Then what?"

"It'll be the hardest thing I've ever done short of leaving her. But I won't see what happened to me happen to you or her, and I won't risk losing her again."

"You know there's no doubt my lion wants her, but until she accepts me, this could be dangerous for her."

"No. It won't. I'll protect her from you and herself. Until she accepts what she is and realizes your lion is also what she needs, I won't take issue with it. But she'll have to want you and accept you before I can deal with the two of you being together. Can you wait?"

"I've seen what it's been like for you. Geez, Bryan, I'm afraid. What if her cat didn't imprint on me. What if she can't accept this?"

"You catch her scent around you? I've already seen the way she looks at you. Think about it—she protected you from me. That had to mean something."

"Hell, I could go rogue."

"You won't. You'll hold out. You're stronger than I was, and I haven't lost it yet. I'll take care of you like you did me." Bryan hesitated and ran his hands through his hair, making it stand on end. "But you have to wait…you know…before you and Lacey…" He hesitated and sighed. "She and I have things to settle between us."

"Hey man, I understand. Only, I'm not as strong as you think." Hunter stared at Bryan long and hard. "Don't wait too long. If her scent gets any stronger I won't be able to hold back."

"Stop worrying. I trust you." Bryan clapped his brother on the shoulder, shoving him in front of him. "Follow her. Let's go talk."

"No." The rumble rose inside Hunter's chest. He stopped and looked toward the grotto then back toward the cave entrance. "I can't do it. My lion is pushing me to claim her. I better take care of the horses and go hunt."

"You gonna be okay?"

"Yeah, for now. You take care of your mate. When she needs me, I'll be there for both of you." Hunter looked back toward the grotto. "And Bryan? Don't worry. I won't claim her until she wants me. Like I said, I want her to want me."

"I won't let her fuck you if it's just about you. This has to be her need or nothing."

"But really, will she accept all this? The shifting? You? Me?"

Bryan chuckled. "Lacey's a scientist. With enough evidence she'll turn us into a study."

"I'm not sure how I should feel about that." Hunter grinned. "I guess it depends on how much is sexual."

# Chapter Twelve

Lacey's feelings for Bryan were mixed, understandably, considering their history. She was still angry, but she couldn't deny being attracted to his sexual magnetism. His voice, his scent, and the way his eyes caressed her when he looked at her reminded her of how they had once felt about each other—how, if she was completely honest with herself, she still felt.

Hunter was a different issue entirely. There was an underlying connection between them making Lacey prickly as hell. Some undeniable attraction drew her to both men. She had to admit Bryan's brother was hot, yet Hunter's appeal confused her.

What had gotten into her? She never wanted anyone after Bryan. Since meeting Hunter, she sensed he'd be able to please her well, and she might enjoy pleasing him right back. After five years of abstinence, for no reason other than she'd had zip for sex drive, suddenly she was ready to jump both men's bones. Both of the men set her blood on fire.

Both? Did she dare allow the fantasy? What would being naked with them be like? The thought made her blush when she envisioned one man at her back caressing her and the other at her breast. Her insides went molten. The thought sent a heated spiral of lust straight to her core where her fingers pressed to ease the aching need. The sensation spiked the need growing within her.

She slouched down in the water, leaned her head against the stones, and let out a long breath.

Visualizing both men touching her made her moan. "Mmm." They'd be just what she needed. Her lips curled into a smile, remembering the way their skin glimmered in the pale light the other evening.

"I hope that smile's for me, babe."

Her eyes popped open. She gazed into the dark, passionate expression painted on Bryan's face, knowing he sensed her arousal. The burning hunger for her was seared clearly on his face. With a voice so rough she could hardly decipher the words through his pleading tone, he offered to replace her fingers.

"Let me, please."

He moved closer, sitting on the lower ledge on her side of the pool. He reached under the water and touched her belly.

"Where's your brother?"

"Don't worry about Hunter. He'll be back when we need him."

"What if…I need him now?"

Bryan's brows rose. "Do you? I'll call him."

He called her bluff.

Lacey lowered her lashes and shook her head. "Not yet." She wasn't ready to have any other man's hands on her. "We have unfinished business."

Bryan exhaled sharply. He leaned over and kissed her, ravishing her mouth as his hand cupped her breast. The texture of his rough palm grazing over her soft nipples felt exquisite. The tips puckered, begging for attention, and he nuzzled her breast with his rough, bearded jaw. He took first one nipple in his mouth and nipped gently, then licked it until she wanted to scream.

She'd been empty too long. Her body, her heart, and her mind needed filling. The pulsing water continued to relax her while his hands and mouth stimulated her.

Her internal muscles spasmed, unable to resist the promise. They longed to embrace his cock, needed to embrace his thick, hard shaft. She wanted the thrust and pressure of a man's cock filling her, claiming her. It had been too long. It felt like it had been forever since a man made her want this.

Lacey reached for Bryan's wrist when he slipped a finger inside her.

"I want to watch you come." His voice sounded raspy, guttural, almost harsh. "I'm so fucking desperate for you—the taste of you, your scent, your warm, tight heat. I know it's been a while for you, so I'll be careful, but I'm not sure I can be gentle."

"Then don't be gentle. Take me. Make love to me, Bryan."

She extended her arms to him, and he lifted her out of the water as if she weighed next to nothing. He was fully clothed and she was wet and naked. He walked her over to the same place where they'd made love the first time and, like that time, he'd already spread a blanket before he joined her.

"I promise I won't hurt you. Never again…if I can help it," he swore.

How did he know those were the words she needed? The truth. The reality of their situation. Her heart clenched in her chest, and her throat tightened when she recognized his concern. Hot tears of happiness filled her eyes and spilled over her cheeks before she could stop them.

Tilting, he kissed her lips, soothing her, licking away the tears from the corner of her lips. “Are you okay with this, Lacey?”

“I’m more than okay,” she said and smiled at him through her tears. “I feel like I’ve been waiting all my life for this moment.”

“No more sad tears.”

“No, no more sad tears. These are glad tears. I’ve never been better.”

She wrapped her arms around his neck and tossed back her head as he pressed his cock against her opening. He inched forward until he was fully encased inside her, and then he began to plunge in and out with short, gentle strokes. Good to his word, it didn’t hurt.

“You feel so tight gripping me this way, so wet and slick, so warm and soft.”

“You fill me completely and it feels so good.”

“Can you take more?”

“More,” she gasped.

He angled her hips and thrust.

She cried out, “Oh, yes. Harder.”

Within seconds his hips bucked with greater force. He grew more desperate, and the strong tremors of her own orgasm teased at the surface as she drove back against his momentum, joining him in the dance.

“Bryan, you’re like an itch I’ve been needing to scratch for a long while. Fill me up and take me harder.”

Like a compressed spring, her body quivered with coiled tension, wound ever so tightly, ready to snap.

“Hang on. Oh, God. Lacey. I. Love. You.” Each word was punctuated with his thrusts—thrusts like nothing she'd ever experienced with him before. Pleasure welled up inside her, and she whimpered.

"I'm coming… Oh, God, Bryan."

The erotic sound of skin slapping against skin brought back memories of them when they were young, desperate lovers. She relaxed, savoring the slippery slide of their sweaty bodies against one another. The intense pleasure heightened with the force of the untold power within him.

He pistoned faster, moving over her at a frantic pace until she felt his cock clench and release. Jets of warm creamy liquid shot inside her with his final thrusts, and she tried to angle her hips to take more of him.

"Be careful. Don't move, yet," he warned.

"Why?"

"I don't want to hurt you."

She stayed still as he cleared his voice. "Uh-hmm. I experienced other transformations. Some changes don't always revert back when I do."

He looked uncomfortable trying to explain. "My cock…is different. It changed when I did."

"Mmm, it feels really big and hard. Sooo good." Caressing his nipples to points, she sucked one between her lips. The way he reacted said he liked it as much as she did and his gratifying groan pleased her.

"Yeah well, there's that," he said, smiling. "But there's a little something else. When I'm ready to come, my cock may be more than you bargained for. The ridges swell to bring on your orgasm, and I can't pull out until they recede."

He lifted her chin and looked for a response. "Freaky?"

"Oh yeah, maybe a little unexpected when you put it like that, but you do know I'm a biologist, don't you? Reproduction is one of my specialties."

"Sure—" Just then, Bryan moved inside her.

"Damn, you feel good filling me." Lacey clenched her internal muscles and felt his erection swell inside her. God, he felt enormous.

"So…you're not freaked out?"

This was Bryan inside her. What he was and who he was, was everything she'd once loved. And he was hers. Always had been. They belonged together. She would never allow him to feel uncomfortable about what happened to him.

"Hey, you're a lion." She grinned and shook her head once. "The size and the stamina come with the territory. Thank goodness you don't bite or come in eight seconds." She stared at his teeth. "You don't bite, do you?"

"What—? No, not when I'm in human form. What's the deal with coming in eight seconds?"

"Oh. Lions have intercourse repeatedly for hours, but coitus is quick. The male lion comes in about eight seconds and stays inside the female to ensure his sperm fertilizes her. Then he comes again and again. Their foreplay involves biting, spitting, and a lot of growling and hissing. The act of sex between cats is combative. They both want it, but they fight all the way through it."

"Hell, there are still some perks to being human. I plan on lasting a lot longer than eight seconds." He kissed the side of her neck and nibbled. "How's this feel?" he asked as he thrust inside her.

"Mmm, wonderful."

He was still rock hard and thick, filling her and

making her want more. There was also that damn itch she needed to have scratched. Again. Maybe they were more like their lions than she wanted to believe.

"I'm close to another orgasm, big guy. I think if you just twitch, you could send me to the stars again."

She clenched her pelvic floor muscles, and he did better than twitch. He thrust until the world exploded around both of them. The aftermath left her feeling like a puddle of orgasmic jelly.

Lacey called out his name on a prayer, and they both murmured a binding oath. "Damn, Bryan. We did it again. Didn't we?"

He chuckled and then brushed his lips over hers. "Hell, yes. Apparently, we're destined for each other."

"If we hadn't fulfilled the pledge before, we did just now."

"Thank God. Lacey, I promise to bind you in love every time." Bryan carried her back to the spring and deposited her into the soothing water.

"Hunter needs me, though. Doesn't he?"

"Yes." Bryan's eyes narrowed, and Lacey heard the low rumble roll through his chest. "He doesn't want your pity, though. He wants to please you, but he wants to know you desire him first."

"I completely understand." She almost laughed thinking she felt the same way. "I'm all itchy inside. Needy. Like there's still something missing."

"Do you think your cat imprinted on Hunter because we're from the same litter?"

"There are documented incidents of male lions, siblings, sharing a pride. I guess imprinting on brothers wouldn't be such a far-fetched notion."

"As much as I'd like to wrap you up and keep you

for myself, my lion won't let me deny you anything you need. If it's Hunter, I'll go get him for you."

"But, Bryan..." How could she refuse to help Hunter escape his lunar nightmares? Besides. She liked him. That was a start. She could see a day when they would truly love each other, be in love with each other and not just in lust. But not yet. "I don't know if I'm ready for...that."

"Well, why don't you let me help you decide?" The sound of Hunter's deep voice right beside her caught Lacey off guard.

He was naked and glorious. His thick erection bobbed against his abdomen. Desire for him pooled like liquid heat between her thighs. This sudden attraction she was experiencing seemed too complicated to settle with a quick "no thank you" to him. Was she ready to let pride and her inhibitions stand in the way of their mutual satisfaction? Of her future and his?

"Try. See if he's what you need to complete you." Bryan's jaw flexed. He inhaled slowly and briskly kissed her.

"Bryan?"

"It's okay. I'll be just outside if you need me."

"But... Bryan, I love you."

"I know. And it's only because I love you that I can do this."

Bryan turned and walked away, this time shimmering into his cat as he disappeared into the dark and Hunter climbed in to the bubbling water.

When he sat down beside her, he brushed a stray lock of hair from her forehead and tucked it behind her ear. Cupping her face in his hands, he looked deep into her eyes and begged, "Lacey, please. Let's see if this is what you need—what we all need. You say stop and I'll stop at any point. Okay?"

"O–okay." Would allowing him to touch her and start something she knew could end badly be a mistake? "Hunter…I've never been with…anyone else."

"I know, darlin', but I have something for that itch, Lace." He took her hand and placed it on his rock hard cock then kissed her, slowly murmuring a warning against her lips, "Somethin' in addition to what Bryan can provide, and I'm afraid you're gonna need this by the next full moon."

## Chapter Thirteen

Hunter wasted no time trying to convince Lacey she would need him, as well as Bryan, when her time came. He sat back and smiled a predatory grin, his attention flicking to her breathless arousal as her breasts bobbed above the water. There was no doubt in Lacey's mind he knew what his perusal was doing to her.

Hunter continued to stare at her, licking his lips. He watched and obviously enjoyed the way her nipples contracted within her areolas. The damn things just begged to be sucked, and the tighter they got, the more he grinned.

"You've got great breasts, Lacey. Big nipples that pucker up into long, tempting nubs. Nubs I want to suck and nip."

He filled his hands with both her breasts until the excess spilled over the top, and he nipped one taut nipple making her gasp out loud. Then he accommodated her need to be touched. He sucked one while teasing the other then switched until Lacey groaned.

"Hunter, just so you know," she choked out, "I'm not feeling one iota of pity for you."

"Bryan told you?"

She nodded.

"Good. I'm not a man who wants pity," he said. "Tell me what you like, Lacey, and I'll give it to you."

"I'm aching for your touch."

Hunter chuckled. "I'll do my best to touch you everywhere. Let me know if I miss any place."

Then he kissed her again.

He tasted familiar but different. Spicy, wild, hot. The effect of his kiss was volatile, like striking a match to dry kindling. She opened for him and kissed him back, tangling her tongue with his as he tried to tongue fuck her mouth. His hand stroked down her throat and cupped her breast. He squeezed lightly. The contrast of his aggressive kiss and his tender touch distracted her.

Lacey imagined heat sizzling the water around them as he played with her tits—touching them, pinching and teasing them as if he knew exactly what she needed. He pulled back then, at first, touched his lips gently to hers, and, as he did, his fingers explored her pussy. Stroking, separating, exploring her folds, until he located her clit, and then he pressed firmly. The pressure aroused her even more.

Bubbles caressed her everywhere, skimming over all her sensitive nerves while the man coaxed another orgasm from her. Pinching her nipples harder, tweaking her sensitive clit, and sliding three thick fingers deep inside her, he tested her opening.

"Come for me the way you came for him," he insisted. "Or harder. Come on, Lacey, come," he urged as his hands and mouth seemed to be all over her body at once.

This need she was experiencing was different from any arousal she had experienced in the past. This was the fever upon her.

Hunter continued to nip at her earlobe, her neck, and then down to her sensitive nipples. The sensations came close to driving her to madness. Especially when he pressed his big thumb deep inside her and stuck the tip of his forefinger into her rear passage.

She came immediately, this time screaming his name, over and over, and she couldn't help being pleased with the satisfaction she saw in his expressive eyes before she dropped her forehead to his magnificent chest and relaxed against him.

Hunter continued to caress her hips, dipping his long fingers between her ass cheeks, touching each sensitive intimate spot. "When we're all together, and you're ready, I'm going to take you here while Bryan fucks your pretty pussy. You want that, Lacey? Having us both inside you, filling you, scratching that itch?"

He liked the way she blushed and didn't answer, but she lifted her head and nodded. Thank God! She would be open to the ménage.

"I want to touch you this time, Hunter. Will you show me what you like?"

"Sure. Go ahead, Lacey. I'm all yours. But I can guarantee I'll enjoy anything you do. Just looking at you pleases me."

"Good. Get out of this water so I can explore and learn all I can about satisfying you." Lacey grinned and stood up. Her wet, golden skin glistened in the lamplight.

"You're the most exquisite woman I've ever seen."

"Aw. You're prejudiced by your cat."

"No. Not my cat. *I* think so, and I did the minute I first saw you, before my cat ever imprinted on you."

"Well, then, thank you." She cupped her breasts and held them out to him.

Hunter's jaw clicked as he ground his teeth. He

touched her full globular breasts. God, she was sexy.

"Hunter, I'm glad you like the way I look. Now, allow me to explore the wonders of your body. Sit up on the ledge so I have better access to discover what you like."

He pulled himself out of the water and sat on the smooth, flat rock in front of her as the water sluiced down his body. Her words aroused him, but when she went to her knees between his thighs, his cock turned harder than steel. For the first time in his life his cock took control. Damn, he hoped he didn't come before she touched him.

"Just give me a minute." He touched a finger to her plump lips and caressed her face. Her braid hung around her shoulder and down across one breast. "Let me do this." He lifted the braid and removed the band from her hair. Undoing the design allowed the long golden strands to tumble around his groin when her warm lips kissed the tip of his penis. She licked, and he gave in to desire, pushing his cock past her lips into the deep recesses of her hot mouth.

He tossed his head back and held on for all he was worth as her tongue swirled over his crown. Lacey sucked his shaft deep down her throat, again tempting him to thrust. The warm, wet orifice felt unbelievably good, with her plump lips surrounding him while her tongue stroked his length. The overwhelming need inside his balls built to near explosive levels.

Lacey deep-throated his full length in one slow, smooth, fluid movement, and at that moment Hunter experienced heaven on earth. His mind couldn't focus on anything but the pleasure. But when he opened his eyes and met hers, he realized with a mouth as talented as hers, he should be the one on his knees worshipping her.

She hand-pumped his cock and took him down her throat again, forcing him to tighten his control. He took a deep breath, forking his fingers through her golden hair for better purchase, and held her in place. Her tongue stroked and her lips vibrated over his crown, moaning as if she was eating a decadent dessert. She sucked and paused several times until the pressure behind his balls ached to release.

Hunter gasped, unable to stand holding back any more, and then pulled out. His cock jerked, objecting to being separated from the pleasure. He had barely prevented her from devouring him and bringing him to completion in that tempting mouth of hers.

"Hunter, I want this. You smell delicious." Lacey mumbled, nuzzling his groin. "Let me do this for you—for me. I want to taste you."

She wanted him, but Hunter realized she wasn't ready for complete intimacy. She would do this much, satisfying him and her need for his lion's essence…but no more. Lacey wasn't going to let him fuck her. Not yet.

He should be satisfied knowing she wanted him, needed him sexually in some way at least. With time, she might be able to accept him completely.

"God, Lacey, how could any man resist an offer like that from these lips?"

Hunter leaned over and kissed her, driving his tongue inside her mouth and devouring her. He tasted a hint of his own wild, tangy flavor inside her mouth. Yes, he wanted her to swallow as much of his essence as possible. The more of his taste and scent she experienced, the closer they would become.

Lacey smiled a feline grin, licking her lips when his fingers wound through her hair and he drew her closer to his engorged shaft. “Like I said—I’m all yours.”

Eventually, her lioness would beg to have his cock inside her. Fucking the lioness was the only way to scratch her itch. When the time came, he wanted her prepared for him, but they both had to be ready for the commitment.

Hunter felt the moon’s pull ever since he’d been infected, and it wouldn’t be long before Lacey completed her transition and shifted. Her scent grew stronger, and his skin prickled with need.

He loved her enthusiastic mouth, but his lion was roaring inside him, demanding to take his mate. For her own safety, Hunter gave himself up to Lacey’s ministrations and didn’t hold back when she started bobbing up and down around his cock, building the pressure behind his balls to explosive levels.

“Lace, I’m going to come. If you don’t want to—”

She pressed a finger inside his ass and Hunter lost it. Cum erupted, spewing into her mouth and down her throat while she sucked, swallowed, and licked, not missing a drop.

“I warned you—”

“I told you. I wanted to taste you.” Lacey narrowed her eyes and licked her lips with that sexy feline smile. “You taste wonderful. I feel better than I have in months.”

Her eyes slowly focused on her hand. She still held his semi-hard cock in her fist. Suddenly, she turned aside. With a shy glance up at Hunter she released him.

He wanted to cry at the loss of her touch, but he sensed she wasn't ready for more.

"Are you ready to head back to the ranch?"

She nodded shyly, looking uncomfortable. "Bryan will be wondering…"

"Bryan will know you're okay with me."

"But…he'll be wondering about…us."

"Lacey? Are you okay with us? Because… Hell, I don't know how to tell you this."

"What?" Lacey looked so innocent—so confused.

"Bryan already knows…about this. You're bound to him. He can sense your thoughts, experience your emotions."

"Oh, God." She moaned and covered her face. "Why didn't someone tell me this before?"

"I thought you understood. Don't be embarrassed. He knew what we were going to do."

"Knowing is one thing. Sharing is another. Poor Bryan."

"You must have been linked to his feelings before."

"Yes, I guess. I never quite understood it." She picked up her clothes and got dressed. "We should get back. I need to see him."

"No. Let me do this. I think I know where he is."

# Chapter Fourteen

Hunter rode the Appaloosa and brought along a second horse, tethered behind him.

Bryan wondered what took him so long. It was only a matter of time before his brother found him. He shouldn't have had trouble tracking him since Bryan had listed all the places he stashed clothes for him last week. He'd started that practice anytime they settled in an area so he'd never be caught with his pants off.

Hunter also knew the high cliffs were one of Bryan's favorite places to think.

"You okay, bro? Lacey's concerned." Hunter's deep voice on the trail behind him didn't surprise him.

"I'm fine. I came up here to get away from the two of you. How is she?"

"You don't know?"

Bryan shook his head without looking at Hunter. "I shifted and ran. Put space between us. I needed to be far enough away to avoid the emotions."

"She'll be relieved to hear that. Apparently, she didn't understand your connection. She freaked out when I told her you could sense her feelings."

"When her need pounds at me, it's almost impossible to resist."

"Where did you go?"

"Went hunting on my land—Emma's portion of the Cauldwell spread. Found a rabbit while I sniffed around for clues."

"Find anything else besides dinner?" Hunter asked and then snorted.

"The rabbit was a snack," Bryan said. "I did find some tracks but they were old. The rogues had been out there. Not recently, though. I caught another scent—stench really. Not sure what it was. Definitely not wolf. More cat than dog, though. Nothing else."

"In five years, dust settles. Someone could cover up a town in that time."

"I know. But Lacey wants answers. She'll need them if she's ever going to trust me," Bryan said.

"She's going to need both of us. But Lacey, the woman, isn't ready for a ménage relationship."

"Her transition will be more difficult unless she agrees to accept us together."

"You and I both know that, but…" Hunter lifted a shoulder in a careless shrug. "I'm not exactly sure how she feels about me. For now, the chemistry between our inner cats draws us together, but we don't have the same human connection you two have."

Bryan noticed that despite Hunter's casual attitude, he wasn't taking things as lightly as he made out. Bryan scrubbed his hands down his face. Frustrated. How were they going to manage this?

"Look, Hunter, she and I have history. Good and bad. She's understandably attached to me emotionally, but if her lioness needs us both during her transition, will it matter?"

"No. Neither of us will allow her to go through the pain. We'll ease her through her need. After, she can decide what she wants to accept."

"Her ranch house won't work after she starts the

metamorphosis." Bryan looked out over the hills. "Being out by the grotto and caves seems the best choice after the transition. We stay in the nearby cabin." Bryan smiled. "It's on my property and away from the town and neighbors."

"Sounds like the perfect place to teach her shifting and hunting. Until she learns how to control her body, her change can take over anytime, anywhere," Hunter said. "We need to be prepared."

"Until when? How long, Hunter?"

"The next full moon. Within the month, we have to convince her we're what she wants. A month won't give her time to master her ability to shift, though."

"There's so much to do to prepare," Bryan said. They would have to hide her until she stabilized. "In the morning, I'm filing the papers to take back the ranch land. We'll need the land."

"One of us has to be with her at all times, Bryan. What do you plan to do about taking care of her ranch and the kids' charity? Who is going to take over her riding business?"

"I'll get Keiran to cover the charity for her. Thomas can oversee the horse business. He's got a good mind for making money. Her classes at the university don't start until next month. It'll be close, but I think she'll be able to manage it by then. Anything else, you or I can handle."

"She has to agree."

"Don't count on it. She's highly volatile. So are we, in our present state—at least 'til we establish the ménage bond between us. We have to convince her, in short order, to accept both of us."

"Good luck."

## Chapter Fifteen

Lacey drifted out of her bedroom and curled up on the couch.

"Mmm, the heat feels good for a change, but I'm so sleepy I could take another nap." Basking in the sun with her head on one arm, she looked up with those slanted cat eyes all rounded, innocent, and questioning. "Would you mind?"

Bryan shook his head. What he really wanted to do was blanket her with his own body. "No, you go ahead. Rest. You'll need your strength."

"Mmm, thanks," she purred, but Bryan's insides jerked awake when she smiled with the sultry, catlike features superimposed beneath her own lovely ones. The lioness's full potential hadn't emerged yet, but he was captivated watching her transformation. Lacey was so amazing he wondered if he'd survive her full transformation.

Soon her slumbered breathing turned to muffled snores. She kept shimmering back and forth between her human and mountain lion forms without truly taking on the lioness. It was hard to keep track of what she'd do next. For the moment, she claimed the one sunny spot in the room and curled up—human, naked, and sexy as hell.

Bryan picked up a blanket and cautiously covered her.

As they waited for the miracle of the transformation to complete, Bryan watched over her while Hunter sorted through the meager supplies they found in her kitchen.

"Thomas said her appetite's been lousy."

"Well, that'll all change when she wakes up. This time she'll be hungry—ready for red meat."

Bryan remembered the hunger—the lack of control. Lacey would be ravenous for a week.

"Then for all our sakes, you better fix a meal out of what she's got on hand until I can hunt up something more substantial."

"Yeah, good thinking. I'd rather not be dinner," Bryan said.

He found what he needed in the freezer and fried up some burgers. There were a few cans of chili in the pantry. He opened two and poured them into a pot to simmer until she woke.

His own stomach growled. "Guess I'm hungry, too."

"You eat something before she wakes up and toss me a burger." Hunter sniffed the delicious aroma wafting through the kitchen and glanced at Lacey through the doorway. She was still sleeping soundly. "I should go hunt up something more substantial."

"Go ahead. I'll be fine here with her."

Lacey stretched out, moving to her side with a hand beneath her head. Looking more like an angel than the dangerous mountain lioness she was, she practically purred in her sleep. When she let out a deep rumble, Bryan looked at Hunter, acknowledging the danger with a knowing nod. Just because she looked human didn't mean she was. During transition, residual feline traits would keep appearing without warning.

Instead of filling him with apprehension, the fact seemed to increase his interest. Maybe it was the cat inside him that was attracted to her wild side. Even knowing any moment she could shift and eat them for lunch, he couldn't help responding to their bond. And he wasn't alone. She had Hunter aroused, too. Being a lion's snack should have been a sobering thought. Apparently, certain parts of their anatomy had minds of their own.

"Fuck this! We need to feed her this for now." Hunter ordered, handing Bryan the burgers he'd cooked.

Before he pulled off his jeans, he said, "Remember, be careful while I'm gone. She'll want fresh meat, and I don't want her eating the horses when she wakes up."

"Don't worry. I'll be extra careful." Bryan glanced at Lacey's fingernails, noting that they'd grown while she slept. "I know how unstable she is right now."

As an afterthought, Hunter asked, "Will you be able to resist her if I leave you two alone?"

"Our bond connects us. It should soothe the animal lust. You said I'll be safe as long as she's sexually satisfied while she goes through the remainder of her transition."

"You sure you can handle her?" Hunter asked.

"Oh, I can handle Lacey."

"Yeah, I know that. But remember, she's not the old Lacey. Our little kitty is at a dangerous stage. Take care."

"I'll distract her with an orgasm or two if I have to."

Lacey rolled over on her back and stretched. Her

nails bit into the mattress and shredded the sheets as she released a growl.

"Better wait for me. It may be too late." Hunter shrugged out of his shirt and tapped a warning on Bryan's chest. "Don't touch her without me if she shifts again, no matter what. We can't risk mating her alone yet."

"Okay, okay, I get it. Stop worrying and go hunt up dinner." Bryan's skin rippled, and his canines lengthened in his mouth at the thought of warm, red meat.

Hunter removed the rest of his clothes before he shifted, and Bryan watched his brother's skin fur up with a glossy golden coat over his massive frame. Growing larger, the sound of his bones crunching was almost deafening in the quiet room. His defined chest exploded into the massive lion's before he dropped to all fours. The facial markings on the lion's face were unique to Hunter and his intelligent gaze stared out of the cat's eyes.

The Were form when he assumed it at the next full moon would be larger, more dangerous. The tables had turned. Hunter's beast could turn rogue at the height of the full moon if the three of them couldn't reach a mutual agreement regarding their unusual predicament.

In any form, man, mountain lion, or Were, Bryan noted his brother's usual sunny disposition had disappeared. His rounded eyes were replaced with the worried scowl Bryan often wore. The Were virus was already taking its toll on his brother.

He and Hunter were on equal ground. When Bryan turned Were–larger, more unpredictable, and deadlier than any other shape-shifter—there hadn't been a power strong enough to stop him unless it was another WereCat or unless he was confined.

Now that Hunter was infected, they'd be a formidable force against the rogues—especially since they'd both found their mate. All Bryan had to do was accept the idea of sharing Lacey and hope she could have feelings for Hunter. Bryan didn't think either Lacey or Hunter wanted a purely sexual ménage relationship. Both of them needed the passionate link that accompanied a true mate bond.

Five minutes later, Lacey's tail flicked around his ankles.

Damn! Hunter wasn't due back yet and she'd shifted—again. Her sleek, soft body wrapped around him. The purr was deeper, a low hum, but genuinely seductive and telling.

Her cat was drawing his lion to the surface. He tried to hold back but he could feel his change threatening. Lacey's slow, seductive moves snaked around him, her scent enveloping him. Her pheromones filled the air. He dared not breathe. Inhaling would draw in more of her scent and bring out his lust. If his cat emerged, there'd be no stopping him.

Bryan's rational thoughts dulled. He remembered something Hunter said about staying away from her sexually. But as she continued to rub her body sinuously against his and nuzzled his crotch with her nose, there was no doubt what she wanted, and Bryan was having a hard time denying his mate what she craved.

His nails turned into claws, and his body hair elongated. Stop. He had to stop himself from changing and bring her back.

She nudged him again.

It was too dangerous—for him and for her—and he wasn't comfortable with the lioness in his human form. When he tried to push her back gently, she jumped up and placed her enormous paws on his chest.

The effect of her being so close made him gasp. He inhaled and felt the change burst from him like an explosion. She head butted him, dropped down, and turned tail. The lion roared and the lioness growled. His mate's sexual need pulled the lion right out of him.

Lacey looked over her shoulder and flicked her tail at him. He pounced on top of her, holding her neck gripped firmly between his massive jaws. Her nails had scraped his shoulder and a drop of his blood dripped on her neck, reminding him to ease up. She hissed at him, but he held her smaller body beneath his, and she finally stilled as he straddled her. Her snarl warned him to be gentle.

Through the miasma of lust and the scent of Lacey's arousal, Bryan managed to regain control over the lion and shifted. At the same time he ordered Lacey to shift back into her human body. For a moment he didn't think she could do it, but then suddenly he had her human body wrapped within his embrace—her smelling irresistibly of cat and woman, her skin feeling silky and hot. His body vibrated with need.

He was out of control and frightened. He wanted her badly.

She purred beneath him. He inhaled, taking in her scent. The pull between mates was too strong to resist. Bryan picked her up, bent her over the bed, spread her thighs, and buried his face in her pussy. He licked her then drove himself into her hot, wet channel. At first she snarled, then purred and called out his name repeatedly as he mercilessly thrust into her, slapping against her ass as he pounded his cock deeper and deeper inside her.

Her image kept morphing beneath him—lioness to woman, woman to lioness. He couldn't focus enough to hold one form either or the other himself. They were mate shifting—as humans and cats—in unison—experiencing the true bond between shifters.

"Get off her, Bryan. I warned you not to fuck her without me."

Bryan glanced over his shoulder without moving away from the lioness. Hunter growled from the door and dropped a bloody carcass at his feet.

Bryan sniffed the air. *Blood.*

Human, naked, and angry, Hunter crossed to the bed where Bryan and Lacey were still engaged. Hunter shoved him. "I said, get off her. You like playing with danger?"

Hunter waited while Bryan tightened control long enough to slowly withdraw from her, careful not to hurt her before his lion fully overwhelmed his humanity. He kept pushing at Bryan until he finally roared and rolled off Lacey.

Fresh meat.

Bryan wouldn't be able to hold back his lion, not with the smell of blood and flesh overpowering Lacey's scent and the smell of sex.

When Bryan lifted his head and stared at Hunter with his lion's eyes, it was only then Hunter realized his brother and Lacey were both mid-shift. Neither was fully engaged in either form.

Bryan was the first to lose it. He and Lacey both

shifted into two huge mountain lions while Hunter held his breath waiting to see how far removed from their human forms they'd gone.

Finally, the smell of raw meat won out. Distracted, Lacey turned, squirmed away, and swiped at Bryan. He followed her to the carcass. Rushing straight toward the kill, the cats' snarls erupted as the scent of fresh game and blood overcame their sexual demands.

The lioness snarled a warning over her shoulder at both Hunter and Bryan before attacking the deer. Occasionally, she glanced up to check their positions. Temporarily appeased as long as they watched, she meticulously feasted on the venison.

For the moment, things looked safe enough. Bryan would never hurt Lacey. Hunter grinned and decided he needed to clean up. Closing the bathroom door behind him, he left the two cats to work things out.

When he returned, she'd allowed Bryan closer. Lacey took a couple of swipes at him when he encroached on her hindquarter, and Hunter grinned as his big bad brother cautiously settled for the venison shoulder.

Lacey finished eating and moved away.

The lioness groomed herself, indifferent to Bryan and Hunter. But within moments, she shimmered back into her human form, her transition seamless.

She sniffed the air with catlike curiosity and headed toward Hunter. Stalking. Investigating. Those slightly rounded, slanted, golden cat eyes stared unblinking and bewildered at him. She approached him as if in a trance, unaware of anything in her surroundings, totally focused on him.

Her catlike grace stunned him. Her beauty took the

breath from him. Lacey was amazing in any form, but she'd become more exquisite day by day as she approached her full transformation. Hunter's cock pressed painfully behind the zipper. His balls tightened, lifting, filling out his pants to capacity.

Lacey's lips parted and her lids lowered in sensual invitation as she stared at his package. Hunter's arm snapped out, snagging her in an embrace, hauling her up against his aching body.

He commanded her, "Unzip me, Lacey. Take me in your hand, now!"

She did that slow feline rub against him and slipped her hand over the straining material. Her hand brushed his cock through his pants, and she tilted her head at him when he moaned. She listened with a sly smile and licked her lips.

Then she pulled his head to hers and kissed him. He swore she purred as she tugged his lower lip between her teeth. She drove him mad.

Hunter nipped her back. Mindless with passion, he growled, "Mine."

The few drops of their blood mingling on their lips would strengthen their bond. It was exactly what Hunter needed. He sucked her lip, gently drawing a drop of her delicious flavor onto his tongue. Mmm, her taste tantalized him. He bent over and nipped her neck, then cupped her chin in his hand and ravished her mouth, fucking it with his tongue.

She explored his mouth with hers and his body with her hands. He sighed in relief, thankful to her for releasing his aching cock from the constriction of his clothes. She stroked his turgid arousal in one hand, while the other hand slid down the inside of his jeans and pushed them down over his hips just enough to gain adequate access between his legs. Carefully lifting his heavy balls from between his thighs, Lacey cupped him and squeezed gently. His balls tightened and lifted in response to the pressure.

He inhaled her scent as she rubbed herself against the length of him. And he enjoyed the moment, allowing her the freedom to explore his body and test his responses.

She lifted his shirt over his head, licked the tight buds of his nipples while he inhaled with pleasure, and then she pulled his pants completely down over his hips. As she dropped to her knees in front of him, he stepped out of his pants and his underwear all in one quick movement. Her hot, moist mouth encompassed his shaft, and the groan of pleasure he'd been holding back with his breath escaped as pleasure zinged through him.

Her fingernails moved up to tease the trail of hair above his groin and slid slowly down his shaft, over his balls, to the sensitive spot behind. Sliding a wet finger between his ass cheeks, she found his tight opening. She massaged the opening, ringing the hole with her fingertip, then entering him with one finger when he relaxed against her hand. The unbearably sweet pressure she applied caused the fluid to pearl at his opening.

He grabbed her hands to still them, struggling for control. She fought him, rubbing the leaking pre-cum bead over the tight crown of his growing erection. As she played with the tip, he sizzled, thickening to an unbelievable size. His breath came rapidly while he fought his release. If he fucked her feeling like this, he'd have to be careful to prevent the lion from taking him over.

Throughout the entire experience, he never relaxed. He couldn't take his eyes off Bryan as he watched them. The mountain lion's interest, as he observed Lacey and Hunter, turned more intense. The closer Hunter came to orgasm, the closer Bryan came to breaking free of his animal spirit.

"Shift, dammit!" Hunter demanded. "I need your help."

Bryan's human form flickered occasionally, darkened narrowed pupils superimposed with his light golden irises. The great mountain cat's face fluctuated—lion to human and back.

"Hurry, Bryan! I don't know how much longer I can hold back."

Bryan's human image pushed through, becoming clearer and stronger, obliterating the lion. The man materialized where the mountain lion once stood. When all traces of the animal were gone, Hunter let out the breath he'd been holding and sighed with relief.

As soon as he looked into his brother's eyes, he wondered if he'd relaxed too soon. Had Bryan fully shifted back? He was in his human form, but had he completely lost the quality of the predator lurking within him? His eyes flashed with hunger. Was it predatory or sexual? Bryan could still be dangerous.

Hunter lifted Lacey up off her knees and cupped her face in his hands, pulling her body against his. He could turn her away from Bryan and protect her if his brother didn't complete his shift, but she still hadn't fully shifted back from her cat, either. She and Bryan would be completely dependent on him until they took one form or the other. He had to guide them through this.

Hunter turned Lacey within his embrace and sniffed her neck, wrapped both arms around her waist and bent his large, naked body over hers from behind while Bryan firmly established his position up front.

Lacey dropped her head back on Hunter's chest and closed her eyes. She encouraged Bryan to explore her breasts, his hands roaming up the front of her torso, rubbing her peaked nipples, while Hunter's palm cupped her mound.

Hunter's fingers slipped between her folds, drawing out her scent, and then her legs suddenly reacted like wet noodles. Her knees buckled, threatening to give out. Thank goodness the men held her up, sandwiched between them.

Lacey was cocooned in their warm embrace and bolstered by their strength. When she opened her eyes, Bryan was staring at her, his face filled with expectation, and longing still visible in his easy-to-read expression. He nuzzled her breast, licking her nipples and soothing her, supporting her weight with his strength.

Hunter held her around the waist, as he sniffed her hair and kissed her neck. Gently, he stroked her. "Mmm, I love the scent of your skin, the way your stomach muscles twitch when I touch you…here, and the way your rounded hips fill my hands."

His words and actions calmed and stimulated her at once. "This kind of lovemaking is foreign to me—

*Lovemaking*? When had the sex turned into an emotional attachment with Hunter? Her words not only surprised her, but Hunter stilled and Bryan snapped his head up, staring at her, the hope visible in his eyes.

"Is that what this is for you?"

"It's never been anything else with you," Lacey admitted to Bryan.

"But with me...?" Hunter sounded anxious. "Did you mean something's changed?" he asked. "Never mind. Don't answer. I'd rather you didn't second guess your feelings."

Was it? Was that what had happened? At some point during their time together, the sexual actions—although highly erotic—had suddenly become an emotional statement of commitment to both men. Making love? She shrugged, turning her gaze from one brother to the other. "It felt different. As much as I thought it would be just sex, Hunter fills my heart much the same way you do, Bryan. It feels like love."

There had always been a special connection between her and Bryan, but she sensed a new attachment growing between her and Hunter. Emotional ties bound them even if they were steeped in great sex.

Hunter spoke first. "Let's get cleaned up."

It wasn't until then Lacey noticed the scratch marks on Bryan's chest and Hunter's hips. She looked at her nails. Had she done that? No, her nails looked normal, short, sensible.

There was blood smeared over one of her breasts, and when she touched her right hand to her neck she felt a warm, sticky liquid. More blood.

Bryan glared at Hunter.

Hunter glared back. He picked her up and whispered, "It's okay, Lacey. Where's the bathroom? We'll clean you up."

Bryan led the way, grumbling as he opened the

door. “It’s over here.”

The day seemed like a dream. Was she imagining she could sense what the men felt, almost what they thought? Perhaps. Another part of her felt like they were leaving something essential out. Blocking her.

“Come on, Lace. You’ll be fine. We’ll explain everything, later.” Bryan urged her toward the shower and turned on the water, making it extra warm. His eyes turned to Hunter. “Set her in while I’ll get her clothes.”

Hunter nodded, and urged Lacey into the shower.

Lacey noticed both men still sported impressive erections despite just finishing with her. “Forget the clothes, Bryan. Why don’t you both join me? You don’t seem satisfied yet, and I believe I could do with another go round.”

Bryan touched a warm, wet cloth between her legs and leaned her back against the wall to bathe her. As she watched his fingers penetrate her folds, she whispered, “So gentle for such a large, gruff man.”

Hunter joined them with another warm, wet cloth and a drying towel.

Lacey groaned as she succumbed to the men’s ministrations. “This feels so good, so decadent, so right.”

“You started your transition.” Hunter spoke quietly, soothing her with the timber of his voice as the words tumbled from his lips. “You’ll be especially sensitive for a while.”

She wanted to pay more attention, but their hands on her body had that itch between her legs returning. They bathed her, and she watched them take turns cleaning themselves off. Each man’s body was a testament to nature’s creation, perfection. Not identical, but nearly. Visually beautiful, and sensually appealing.

Without giving much thought to anything other than touching their aroused members and sucking the tasty cum from them again, she wondered what else mattered.

Both men shared a glance and Bryan said, "Just a minute, Lacey. Try to focus while we tell you what's happening."

"Okay." She smiled, staring at all that delicious skin. "I'm focused."

Bryan held her as Hunter stepped away from them.

She tensed in Bryan's arms as he whispered, "We're bound to one another, Lacey. The fevers, the fainting, and the inability to form relationships with anyone else, are all part of your change."

She shook her head from side to side and looked down at her nails. "The marks on your bodies? I did that?" She frowned.

"No big deal. It's part of mating for us. Like you once told me, mating between cats is a contact sport. We heal quickly. The lions are who and what we are."

"No big deal? Scratching you like that may be nothing to you, but turning into some kind of Were-shifter bound to both of you is a big deal for me."

Hunter stepped out of the bathroom, wrapping a towel around his waist and returned to the bed. He took Lacey in his arms. "You're ours. Until you felt the conversion coming over you, we weren't sure that Bryan had actually infected you."

"I checked with my father at first. Then when I didn't trust him to tell me the truth, I called Thomas."

"That's right, you contacted Thomas… Your father knew where you were all along and let everyone believe I'd sent you off?"

"First thing you should know is that Thomas is a vampire. I figured no one would mess with him, including my father."

"Vampire. There are vampires, too?" Lacey's head whipped around as she fought back the sense of betrayal and jealousy. Thomas was her friend and had never indicated he and Bryan shared secrets.

"I know what you're thinking. Stop. Neither of us could share our issues with you back then. The only reason I contacted him was because I've known about him since he reached maturity and turned."

"Jack called today. Do you want to know what he found?"

"What?" she hissed, but then relaxed when he wrapped his arms around her.

"My father and Tory had a motive to keep me away. The land. Jack found out Tory's mother is a jaguar shifter from New Orleans. When your father went looking for me, she killed him to make it look like I was dead, like we'd both been attacked by wild animals."

"Bitch." Lacey snarled and her nails elongated as her fingers curled into paws. "Oh, no! What's happening?"

"Try not to get too upset." Bryan soothed her, running a hand across her cheek. "This is all what should be happening, but I want you to take it slowly."

"What's wrong with me?"

"Nothing," the two men said in unison.

"Absolutely nothing," Hunter added as Bryan said, "We think you're perfect."

"A perfect what?"

"Mate, woman, mountain lioness." Hunter was beginning to grow on her.

He certainly knew how to say all the right things to a…lady? His charm must be why she wasn't more upset by the recent revelations. Maybe this explained everything—the way she felt for Bryan and her new, deep feelings for Hunter.

Lately, she'd been feeling different about a lot of things. Relief swallowed up her anticipation. This was a good reason why she could even contemplate a relationship with two men…uh…shifters.

## Chapter Sixteen

The once icy core inside her body melted into liquid fire while the men's hands seduced her.

Bryan's fingers played with her clit, strumming rapidly. Hunter's fingers inside her pulled her thick cream out, smearing it all over her rear entrance. Hunter pressed in and out, circling, penetrating a fingertip at a time, inch by slow inch, preparing her rear muscles for his size.

She pressed against the single finger seeking purchase in her rear hole and groaned as she felt an arousal unlike any she'd ever known. Tingling, prickling sensations traveled over every inch of her skin.

Sandwiched between two massive chests, Lacey gasped as Bryan pinched and tweaked her nipples until she could feel the pull deep inside her hot, wet cunt. Every time Hunter ringed her tiny rear hole with her slippery juices, she wanted him to press his cock deeper into her forbidden entrance while Bryan pushed his beautiful cock into her vagina.

The brothers finger-fucked her, thrusting up and inside her, finding every bundle of nerves, and stimulating her until she wanted to scream. If somebody didn't fill her with cock soon, she'd explode.

Just when she thought she might find that moment of satisfying bliss that seemed to have eluded her lately, they stopped, pulling out, leaving her empty.

"She's so wet the moisture is dripping all over her pussy and ass."

Bryan placed his big hands on her hips and pressed her soft mound against his hungry cock while his brother held his body against hers from behind.

Hunter had his thick cock in hand, teasing her back entrance with it. In an inch, then out, until she wanted to scream or impale herself on him.

Oh, if only they would penetrate her instead of continuing this pleasurable torture. The feline itch reached unbearable proportions, the pressure too great to endure much longer. She needed to be filled, she needed thrust, she had to come. Groaning, she grabbed Hunter's ass with one hand and wrapped her other around Bryan's neck.

She whimpered out a whispered plea. "Now, please, Bryan, please, Hunter." She felt the growl at her neck as teeth pierced the tender flesh where her neck met her shoulder. Both men held her, marking her simultaneously. Hunter's cock penetrated her ass, filling her. The sensation stretched her limits. The feeling was similar to the first time Bryan took her virginity. The tight stretching sensation sent chills through her, filling her with satisfaction. Goosebumps covered every inch of her skin before she erupted in the first of several orgasms.

Bryan thrust into her tight, wet channel up to his balls, filling her, and together the men surged inside her.

She gasped. Ripples of pleasure undulated through her as they pumped inside her, scratching that relentless itch, demanding her release with their bodies.

Their words swirled inside her head—words promising love, pleasure, and devotion forever and more. She sensed something wonderful building inside her, but she didn't understand.

*Come*, the voices urged, *come. Let go. Come for us.*

She seemed to rise higher and higher, twirling faster and faster, getting closer and closer to some point—an unknown goal.

Spiraling out of control, a violent explosion threatened to erupt from somewhere inside her. Wound up tight as a spring, she didn't think she could take any more, and then the first orgasm came—a shattering release—followed by another. One after another, the three of them climaxed as one, each experiencing everything the others felt. Her body continued to convulse. The men were unable to pull their cocks free from her body while her internal muscles pulsed, clenching their cocks, milking their ejaculate from them with her after-spasms.

Heat.

Chills.

Molten lava.

Shimmering crystals of pure pleasure.

The experience was the most perfect moment she'd ever encountered.

Lacey wasn't even self-conscious as the men intently watched the thin liquid pump from her pussy in steady streams. Female ejaculate. As far as Lacey knew, so few forceful orgasms produce female ejaculation, they were seldom documented. Until that moment, she believed they were a fallacy, but now that she'd had one, she made a mental note it wouldn't be the last.

"Oh my God, I experienced the impossible dream—a female ejaculation and multiple orgasms."

There would be no going back to anything less than the pleasure these men could bring to her. Lacey understood that now. Because it wasn't just sex. It was a connection between the three of them she couldn't deny.

"At least two." Hunter nuzzled her neck and chuckled. "Don't sound so surprised."

"No, actually three or four, maybe five times," she corrected Hunter. "And why shouldn't I be surprised?"

"Because that's how it always is with bonded mates."

"So, Bryan, we're bound for life? Like Hunter says?"

"Uh…yes, afraid so."

"How do you really feel about this…ménage relationship?"

"Honestly? I thought I'd be more jealous, but I love watching you come like that. God Lacey, the way you orgasm with both of us inside you is so powerful… I want to feel your pleasure like that every time. I want us to take you every way and please you so much the earth shakes."

"Don't worry. I'm going to keep you both so busy." Lacey grinned, accepting Bryan's explanation. *Wow!* How could a woman refuse an offer like that? But there were Hunter's feelings to consider. "What about you, Hunter? What do you want?"

"I can't deny the sex is awesome, but…"

"What?" Lacey said. "You can tell me. I won't get my feelings hurt." *Maybe.* She loved him. Even if she hadn't said the words, the feeling was there inside her, ready to shatter if he couldn't love her back. There was already a fist of dread clenching her heart.

"Lacey, I want you to learn to love me the way you love Bryan. Do you think that will ever be possible?"

The grip around her heart released. "No. You're not Bryan. But, Hunter, now that I have come to love you, it is entirely like loving you, not like anyone else. It's not even the bond. You know I liked you well enough before, so the loving you now part seemed to blossom. But I would want you to return my feelings before you committed to our relationship—"

"That shouldn't take much," Bryan said, grinning like the Cheshire Cat. "Especially since he's been ga-ga over you since you brought me to my knees on the dance floor. He's a sucker for your feisty nature, babe."

Hunter shrugged his shoulders and stared at her with the same stupid, self-satisfied smile plastered on his face, and then he kissed her, taking her breath away. "Not bad. What do you think Bryan, can she handle both of us?"

"Oh, you two think you were that good—"

Hunter opened his eyes wide. "You did compare us to deities—"

"It was a figure of speech, something one screams in the throes of passion. You can't hold me to anything I said in the heat of the moment."

Okay, so maybe she promised to do anything for them if they just didn't stop touching her. Maybe she had sobbed out their names, along with a few expletives, several vows…and yes…she had compared them to a couple of virile gods.

"All right!" she admitted. "You were good." They cocked their heads at her. "Great. You were excellent," she sighed.

Too late. She wondered how to keep their heads from swelling. Both men were pretty self-confident as it was. When she saw the expressions on their faces change, she understood how much her approval meant to them, and her heart melted. They'd brought her so much satisfaction. Their response put a different twist to her plans.

"I see you're pretty proud of yourselves. Now it's my turn." She rubbed her hands together like she was ready to take on a challenge. "I'm going to make you boys scream with pleasure until you come harder and longer than you ever have."

She wished she had a camera to document the looks on their faces. Bryan's eyes went all heavy lidded and seductive. But, beneath the surprise on Hunter's face, she detected a slight challenge. His lips curled in a questionable smirk. "Bring it on, babe. I'll bet fifty you're screaming first. Right, Bryan?"

"Sucker bet, Hunter. Don't make it," Bryan warned with his hands raised in surrender. "Been there. Done that. Can't wait to go there again. I know she can make good on her threat. She's made me shout out more than a few times," Bryan admitted with a laugh.

"How hard did she make you come?"

"Don't ask!"

"You were younger then."

"Not really. It was just yesterday she had me hollering like a teenage boy. Besides, she has the advantage now because I can't live without her. Forget it, Hunter. I'm not taking your bet. I've been aching for her for five fucking years. Instead of whacking off into my right hand when I come, I'm looking forward to being buried inside her tight, hot pussy for the rest of my life."

"Well, we'll see," Lacey mumbled and started to turn aside.

Bryan cupped her face in both his hands, forcing her to look up at him. Rubbing a thumb across her lower lip, he lowered his head to her lips. The kiss was soft and tender and his words sounded worried when he asked, "What's the matter, sweetheart?"

No matter how much she wanted this, there was something painful about believing he only wanted her because of their past promises and the bond.

"If you hadn't bound me to you five years ago, you'd have been having sex with other women all this while. Do you think you'd still want me as much?"

"It was never just about the sex. I asked you to marry me before I knew." Bryan leaned his head against her forehead and closed his eyes for a moment before he opened them and stared straight at her. "Lacey, I love you. Always have. Don't make this sound like we don't have other choices. We chose each other then, and I'd choose you again."

"Just checking." She tried to smile back at him in a non-committal way, but the anticipation of pleasure soared straight into both their minds and she winked at him instead.

She turned to his brother and taunted him. "Hmm, so, Hunter, you don't think I can bring you to your knees, begging for release?"

"You'll have to prove it."

The challenge in his grin said she'd have to prove herself to him. The sparkle in his eyes told her he'd enjoy her efforts.

"Here's my final warning. I may not have had a relationship with anyone since Bryan, but the studies I've done with the biological sexual practices of Southwestern mammals has been excellent research. All was applicable to humans."

Hunter had the nerve to laugh. Maybe that was his most engaging characteristic—his lightheartedness. There was definitely something uniquely appealing about him. What she felt towards him was completely different from what she felt for Bryan—not less—just different. Perhaps later she'd examine those differences in greater detail.

She spent years studying Southwestern mammals. After learning everything there was to know about them, she refocused her studies, comparing their reproductive methods with humans. Part of those studies included comparing sexual pleasure. There were many ways to hold off or induce an orgasm. Hunter was going to force her hand to make her point.

"Ready, Hunter? I'm very good at my job."

"Bring it on. Even if I lose, I win."

"We all win," Bryan said, as she pointedly walked toward the bed.

"Three can play this game."

# Epilogue

After their shower, Lacey said, "Let me make love to you both, again."

She'd sworn not to let emotions wreck great sex but she was happy to admit her feelings for Hunter were more than sex—more than the bond.

Hunter ran a finger across her bottom lip. "Don't think about that or anything. Just this." His lids lowered sensually as he took her lips with his. Bryan joined them, wrapping his arms around her, and kissed her neck.

That's when the bond clicked like a lock around her heart. She felt it and gasped.

"What?" Hunter tilted her chin up and gazed deep into her eyes.

"Yes, making love is exactly what this is," she said and kissed them. First Bryan, then Hunter. "I love you both. I need you both. I can't live without either of you." She squeezed them tightly and released them. "And everything feels right when I'm in your embrace."

Hunter took her hand. "Then let's always make love," he suggested as he picked Lacey up and headed to the bed. Bryan was already there waiting with the sheets pulled down.

"Thanks, Bryan, for being able to accept this." When Hunter put Lacey down beside his brother, he stared at her for a long moment before he spoke. "I can't believe I'm so lucky. I swear I fell in love with you the first day I saw you."

"I think Bryan suspected that. You knew then we were meant to be together, didn't you, Hunter?

He nodded. "I tried to fight it, but how would I have lived without you, Lacey?"

"You don't have to." She took his hand and pulled him toward her. He laughed as he toppled onto the bed on top of her. She ran her hands over his chest and kissed her way up his neck.

"Mmm. After we make love together, can we shift? Will you show me how to hunt jaguar?" Lacey asked.

"Yes, you vindictive female. We guarantee you'll find closure for your father's death."

Hunter said, "There's one more thing we should do to complete the bond."

He gave Bryan a telling look, leaving Lacey looking confused. "More?"

"Our lions want to claim our lioness," Bryan explained. His voice went low and gravelly, the lion already affecting him.

Her eyes opened wide with surprise. "You mean we'll… You want to…?"

"We'll mate with you after our shift. My lion is aching to cover you."

Hunter warned her, "It won't be making love, Lacey."

"It will be a claiming," Bryan said. "Are you ready for that?"

A stirring within her told her yes. Her lioness was intrigued by the idea of the dominant males taking her and claiming her. "As long as you admit I claimed you both first."

"Then let the lovemaking begin," Hunter shouted, pulling Lacey into an embrace.

"Wait, Hunter. I have something to ask Bryan first." She moved over and cupped Bryan's face in her hands. "Bryan? Tell me you're okay sharing my love with Hunter. I have to be sure."

"No, Lacey. Love can't be shared. It's given completely. By loving Hunter you won't be loving me any less. You'll be loving Hunter. He's my brother and I love him, too. I can't watch him go through what I've been going through living without you for these past five years." A low growl made his words sound almost mournful.

"That's a beautiful way to look at it, Bryan," she said, as she crawled up his legs. "Sorry I doubted your motives." She scooted down his body and licked her lips. When she reached his groin, she bent to kiss him between his thighs, bringing his balls to her lips, one at a time. "Forgive me?"

Bryan flipped her on her back and straddled her with his stiff cock poking into her belly before she knew what hit her. "Not yet." His growl sounded more playful than threatening. "You can make it up to me later."

"Promise?" she asked.

"Promise!" Bryan laughed then he kissed down Lacey's neck to her shoulders, and lower. He took turns flicking the tips of both of her nipples with his tongue while Hunter moved higher and kissed her lips with a newfound passion.

"Mmm, decadent. Your lips taste like honey."

"You know what's really delicious?" Bryan asked.

"Try her sweet cream filling. Since she transformed, she tastes like dessert all the time. Can't decide which I like more, her mouth or her pussy."

"Hmm, that may be a challenging dilemma. Spread your thighs so I can make my own decision," Hunter said.

"Now, boys," she said. "There's no rush." Lacey giggled. "We have the rest of our lives to argue over my tastiest assets." After she rumbled a purr, she added, "And yours."

As Bryan and Hunter switched positions, Hunter sucked at her breast before moving to her navel and then on to her short, clipped mound, making her gasp at his first touch. He grinned. "I'm undecided. Her tummy tastes good, too. Might have to taste this." Burying his face at her entrance, his tongue whipped across her clit before he lapped at her pussy lips.

Lacey groaned and arched into his mouth. Tremors of pleasure wracked her torso.

"And this." He licked her clit with a long thorough swipe, sending ripples of ecstasy through her body.

"Mmm…and this." His voice grew deeper with his desire and vibrated across Lacey's last nerve. She trembled beneath him as he separated her folds with his fingers before he drove into her with his rough tongue.

She whimpered against Bryan's lips as she pressed her center against Hunter's mouth while she gripped his hair in one hand. Spreading her legs wider, she angled her hips higher to give Hunter better access. Any more and she'd explode.

She cupped her breast as an offering to Bryan when he released her lips. Holding his head to her breast, she watched as he sucked and teased her nipple, turning fingers of desire into heat that spread rapidly through her and melted her insides.

Hunter worked her pussy with his mouth and his fingers, licking and sucking her clit until her orgasm threatened. The pressure inside her built like a smoldering volcano. With a gentle tug at her nipple, Bryan helped Hunter send her over that pleasurable cliff, and Lacey collapsed beneath them, boneless.

She refused to allow her old standards to influence this moment. If Bryan was okay sharing her with his brother, who was she to object? Especially on the heels of the best orgasm she'd ever experienced. A blanket of comfort enveloped her in the form of two male bodies, two men she loved and cared for, and Lacey sighed, content for the first time in a long time. The years of loneliness would have been worth every minute if she could have these two attentive men loving her for a lifetime.

Two men. Thomas would smile with glee when he discovered she'd gone over to the dark side and was in a committed ménage relationship. And the girls? They would be proud to discover she could do some kink after all. Friends like hers were always supportive, and knowing they wouldn't care if they found out she was a part-time mountain lioness set Lacey's mind at ease.

Bryan smiled at Lacey. "Ready?" he asked.

"For what?"

"This." He crawled on top of her and shifted.

When she looked up into the incredible rare smile of the powerful mountain lion, she wasn't afraid. His pale golden eyes lined with ebony looked down at her. Bryan was breathtakingly beautiful in any form. And Hunter lightened her heart as no one ever could.

*And sexy. Don't forget how sexy I am.*

Lacey's shift took a little more effort. *I love you.*

*Me, too.*

Hunter joined them.

*Me, three.*

Lacey followed Bryan and Hunter out the back door into the cool night air, and when the full moon lit up the western sky, the three unusually large mountain lions raced into the hills.

## About the Author

E.L. March (author Eliza March) focuses on the reader's senses with her breathless award-winning romance stories. She loves writing about sunny days filled with flowers and butterflies, and stormy nights immersed in candle-lit bubble baths, listening to haunting music, and drinking Champagne. Reviews claim her characters are three dimensional and her plots uniquely fascinating.

Eliza is living her own romance story with her fated love and her happily ever after.

~*~

Visit E.L. at
www.ElizaMarch.com

~*~

To chat with E.L. March and other Wild Rose Press authors of erotic romance, join us at
www.groups.yahoo.com/group/thewilderroses.

Also Available
from The Wild Rose Press, Inc.
and major retailers.

# The Moon, the Madness, and the Magic

*Enchanted Mountain*

## By E.L. March

Fate sealed Rourke and Dane Grayland's destinies thirty years ago. Now Celeste Cameron, a fae shifter, understands why she's irresistibly drawn to both the Werewolf and the demon dragon shifter. Surely with her succubus nature, she'll be capable of seducing the two alpha men, but will she be able to convince them that sharing her to fulfill the Prophecy would be better than the alternative—chaos, destruction, or death?

Why are the Rourke and Dane's tastes, in everything from food to sex, changing? Maybe because one is the prince of the wolf pack and the other is a dreaded demon dragon shifter and the leader of the Lore. They have one option—accept their destiny and complete the ménage bond or die.

Also Available
from The Wild Rose Press, Inc.
and major retailers.

# Hook

*The Lure of the Mer*

## By Laney Kaye

Marine biologist, Jayde Collins, has a love affair with the ocean. Lucky for her, because lately, swimming is the only way she can get wet without investing heavily in rechargeable batteries. While out diving, she's caught by the crew of a trawler, beaten, and dumped as shark bait. Rescued and magically healed by a hot lifeguard, she's not sure if she's dreaming, but with the erotic fantasy he offers—sex with two men—she's not sure she wants to wake up.

Trent Okeanós leads an elite group of Australian lifeguards who hide a secret; they are the last of the Mer. His law forbids sex with humans unless another Mer joins them, but when he saves Jayde, he's unprepared for the jealousy warring within him. Yet if he dares let his lust turn to love, Jayde will be bonded to him for life and he'll be stripped of immortality.

Thank you for purchasing
this publication of The Wild Rose Press, Inc.

For questions or more
information contact us at
info@thewildrosepress.com.

The Wild Rose Press, Inc.
www.thewildrosepress.com

To visit with authors of
The Wild Rose Press, Inc.
join our yahoo loop at
http://groups.yahoo.com/group/thewildrosepress/

www.ingramcontent.com/pod-product-compliance
Lightning Source LLC
Chambersburg PA
CBHW060941180626
46817CB00004B/1663

* 9 7 8 1 5 0 9 2 2 8 5 9 1 *